Potato Famine Orphan

Published in 2018 by

David Lovell Publishing
PO Box 44 Kew East
Victoria 3102 Australia
tel/fax +61 3 9859 0000
email publisher@davidlovellpublishing.com

Design by David Lovell Publishing
Typeset in 10.5/17 Book Antiqua
This edition printed through Ingram Spark

National Library of Australia card number
and ISBN 978 1 86355 173 1

Full Cataloguing-in-Publication details available from
the National Library of Australia

Potato Famine Orphan

Peter A. Hall

David Lovell Publishing
Melbourne Australia

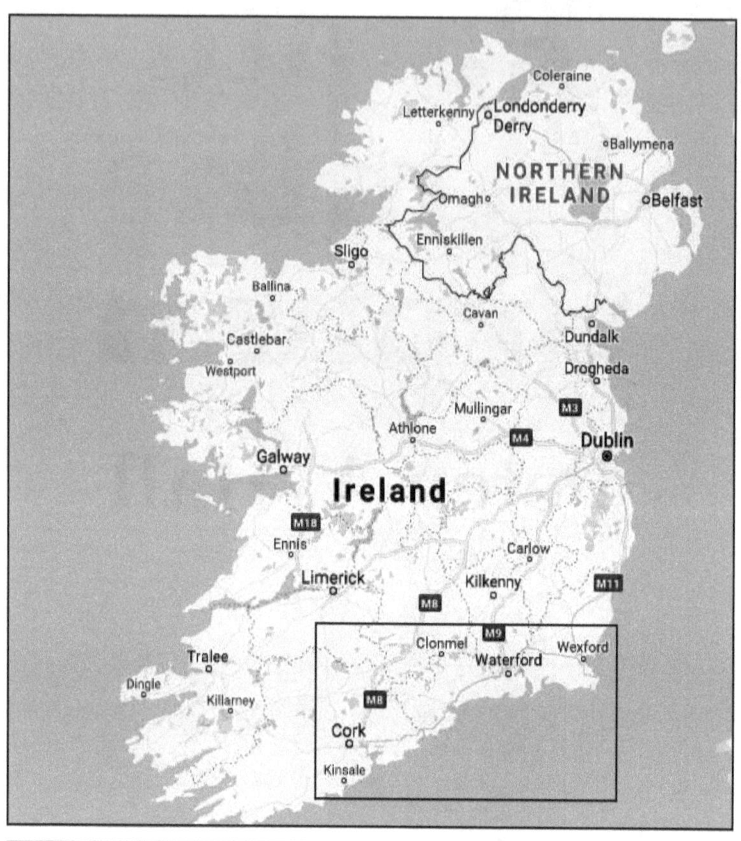

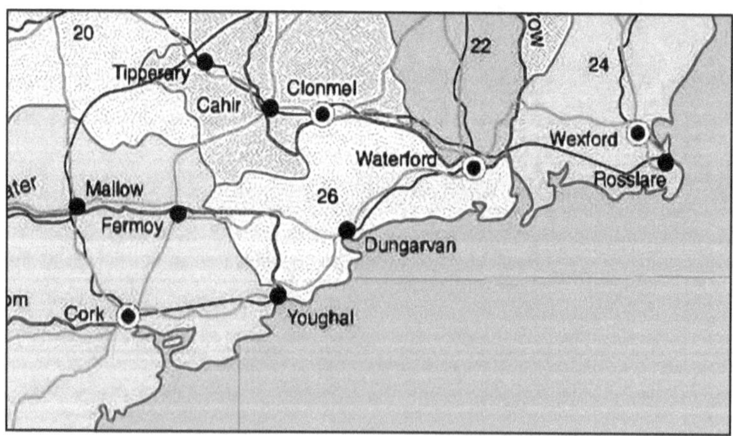

A map of Ireland. Catherine O'Laughlan was unashamedly Irish. She spent most of her early life in Dungarvan, town and harbour of County Waterford. James, her first husband, was born in Cork.

CONTENTS

The front cover

Early this century, Marie and I were visiting the Hermitage Museum in St Petersburg. It was there that we came across a painting of a peasant girl that really captured my imagination. It was the work of Ilya Repin (1844-1930), one of Russia's renowned Realist artists. This painting was at that time on loan from the Irkutsk Regional Gallery of Fine Arts. I fell in love with this humble peasant girl, who subsequently became for me my vision of Catherine, the Irish Potato Orphan, who is the subject of this story. Given that I had no photo of Catherine, maybe you will understand why I chose this particular artwork to represent her.

INTRODUCTION

This is the story of Catherine O'Laughlan, Irish Potato Famine orphan. Catherine was one of thousands of girl orphans who survived the famine and who were given a chance for a new life in Australia. She was the only one of her Irish family to survive the Potato Famine, which led to the deaths of over a million people.

In 1848 Catherine was transported aboard the *New Liverpool* to Australia where she went on to survive a harsh life in the Victorian goldfields, the loss of two husbands, and the loss of five of her thirteen children. She likewise survived hunger, thirst, poverty, floods, bushfires, riots and family tragedy. That's Catherine in a nutshell.

Most of us love a good story. In these uncertain times of threatening nuclear war and economic uncertainty, we look to the past, searching for patterns of resilience and the secrets of survival. Learning about our past becomes a way of defining ourselves, establishing how we fit into history and the scheme of things. We focus on forebears such as that one insignificant human being of Celtic origin – Catherine, our Dungarvan Potato Famine orphan. Celebrating her life is what this story purports to do. In reality it represents one small part of the continually unfolding story of humankind. But, as Catherine's descendants, it is our reality.

How did this story pan out? How did our particular family survive the ravages of time? You are about to find out.

In the Catherine O'Laughlan story, we go back seven generations, before the invention of modern communications, when many could not read and write, and we research the story of our O'Laughlan ancestors. We talk to the older generations, we wade through historical texts and we plumb the depths of the internet. It is amazing what a wealth of information is out there floating around in the ether.

When we have wrung out all possible information from available sources, we still want more. So what do we then do? We create the historical novel. What we don't know, we make up. When you run out of facts, you invent, you extrapolate. You move from the certain, to the probable, and then to the possible. That is precisely what our Catherine O'Laughlan story is – an historical novel or, more exactly, an historical novella – about eighty per cent of which is based on fact.

I believe Catherine, our forebear, ticks all the boxes. Her story includes the whole gamut of human experience – love, dispossession, poverty, virtual slavery, escape, resilience, enterprise, adaptation, compromise, loyalty, hard work and the ultimate inevitability – death. Catherine survived the lot of the landless, and redefined herself as a proactive resilient survivor, who lived a colourful productive life marred by tragedy but with a good dose of success. Above all, she was a survivor.

I gratefully acknowledge the input of Margaret Vrkljan, the initiator, and Margaret Walshe, the researcher, both of whom helped me, the story-teller, celebrate the life of Catherine our great-great-grandmother. It has been a wonderfully exciting ride. I hope you can share my excitement.

Peter Anthony Hall

Beginnings

When we were little kids at school, I'm sure that you like me used to inscribe on the cover of your exercise book a list of those significant details that differentiated you from the other billions of human beings that populate this planet. You began with your name, and then your address – street name and number, then Melbourne, Australia, Planet Earth, Solar System, the Universe. We located ourselves geographically, identifying ourselves on a horizontal axis (the place line) and on a vertical axis (the time line). Where these met, that was you and me (or should I say *I*, because we all know that 'the verb *to be* takes the same case before the verb as after it').

In this story, in similar fashion, we zoom in, Google Earth style, on a young man who didn't have an exercise book, had never been to school, and couldn't read or write. His name was Andrew O'Laughlan. His surname is the first clue. Obviously Irish! We begin our story in the winter of 1822.

Andrew is a carpenter. He is standing in front of a little shack (what the

Irish call a *bothy*) beside a stream that runs into the Colligan River. That's the closest thing he has to an address. No street name! No number! He looks down towards the town of Dungarvan, which is in the valley below about eight miles away. In this story we will use miles, yards, feet and inches, as that's Andrew's language. Napoleon and his metric system have not as yet made an impact on Ireland.

Dungarvan is a port and a quite significant town on the Colligan estuary. So you have never heard of the Colligan River, or Dungarvan? Maybe you'll need your geography book or Google Maps. You will see that Dungarvan is situated in County Waterford, in the south-east of Ireland. It's about sixty miles from Waterford to be precise – 127 miles south of Dublin and 200 miles from the coast of Britain. As to the planet Earth, the Solar System and the Universe, Andrew doesn't have a clue, nor is he particularly interested, as he never went to school. School was prohibited for Irish Catholics by the British authorities as was the ownership of property.

Life's so simple for Andrew. He's not interested in stats or geography. His life revolves around his immediate environment and the people around him. That's the Irish way, particularly for poor Catholic peasants whose focus was on surviving from day to day. Reading and writing were foreign to most of them.

The Colligan Hills, eight miles to the north of Dungarvan, are quite stunning. Andrew wallows in the visual splendour that surrounds him. What a view! He has hills above and around him. To his right is Colligan Wood. And he has his own personal babbling brook that runs into the Colligan River right on the bend. Not a bad bit of real estate! Life's pretty good for a poor carpenter as is Andrew O'Laughlan. Water on tap, a view to die for and timber galore! What more could he want?

How did Andrew come by a five-acre slice of prime real estate snuggling amongst the trees beside this babbling brook? It is what we blithely call the luck of the Irish. It was about whom you know. A friend of a friend and a reasonably congenial absentee English landlord, Sir Wilfred Fortescue, made it possible for Andrew to rent (not buy) this small piece of real estate hidden in the Colligan Hills. Sir Wilfred was an amicable old chap, who treated his tenants well, provided they paid on time.

During the so-called good years, from the 1820s to the '40s, the rent continued to roll in from his several hundred Irish tenant farmers or cottiers. Generally, cottiers were provided with a small cottage and a small piece of land on which to grow crops on a one-year tenancy basis. The cottier paid about two pounds a year for the lease of the land. Often a poor cottier with a farm offering a low yield paid in kind rather than cash. The more profitable products were wheat, barley and oats. In good times, these were cash products, which enabled Andrew to pay the rent on time. The cottier and his family had to survive on potatoes – eight to fourteen pounds per workingman per day. They grew easily in all kinds of soil. That's a lot of 'taters', but the nourishment quotient was significantly less than that offered by the variety of products available to their more affluent Protestant neighbours.

Andrew was a cottier with a difference. His property was hidden in the Colligan woods and without a cottage. By special arrangement, he had the right to clear the land, build his own cottage and use the timber as he wished. Five acres provided an adequate source of timber including a handful of much-sought-after oaks and several lichen-encrusted yew trees.

He won both ways. As he cleared the timber, he built tables and chairs to sell to prospective clients. And while he was at it, over twelve months, he built himself a bothy, a humble little cabin. Andrew's bothy, made of locally sourced materials, was perched on the hillside, snuggling comfortably amongst the trees. The walls were of interlocking, stacked-up, dried-out turf, the rafters were locally sourced pine, and the roof was a mesh of rushes gathered from the Colligan River. What a wonderful start for a young man of twenty-three!

But every red-blooded young man knows that there is more to life than water, work, a modest little shack and a stash of wood. Andrew has hit the jackpot there also. For there is someone in this world who thinks he is the 'ant's pants', and the ultimate cool dude, or whatever other cliché or neologism you want to throw into the mix.

It is springtime, 1823. Thrushes, robins and larks are singing joyously in the woodlands. Love is in the air.

Under a yew tree a few yards away we focus on a young girl, about eighteen years of age. Her name is Mary Kelly. How Irish can you get! But no oil painting! Skinny, flat-chested, scraggy, straw-coloured hair, but with the most beautiful bewitching eyes, and a face full of endearing freckles – and obviously deeply in love with the guy with the hammer and chisel.

No sex before marriage in those days! Father O'Leary is watching. And so is God. Andrew can barely contain himself – a red-blooded, hormone-driven young man of twenty-three. Or is it twenty-four? Andrew wasn't too sure.

Things happen fast. Before you know it, there is a marriage to celebrate. Andrew can't wait, for all kinds of reasons. To hold this girl with the skinny body and the bewitching eyes in his arms, marry her with the blessing of God, and then work at populating Dungarvan with their progeny – this is his all-consuming agenda. Let's do it, he thinks, and fast. Fortunately, Mary Kelly shares his dreams.

It was time for a wedding. Invitations were sent out by word of mouth. There were no written wedding invitations. Few of the locals were literate. But, formal invitations or not, the word got round fast.

The special day arrived. Neighbours emerged from the trees. Donkeys and primitive cartloads of friends and relatives pounded the dusty road. Smiles, tears and gales of laughter pervaded the clearing where the humble nuptials were to be celebrated.

Father O'Leary, standing in for the Almighty, presided in his alb and chasuble. 'Will you take this woman to be your lawful wedded wife?' Andrew, the country carpenter, wanted to shout out the Irish equivalent of, 'My bloody oath!' but he restrained his unruly emotions. In his confident country-boy Irish twang, and with a tremor in his voice, he responded loudly with the appropriate 'I do!' Mary, in similar fashion, with tears welling in her eyes, managed to churn out the same age-old response. She really wanted, country-girl style, to shout out 'Do I ever!' But just like her namesake, Mary the Blessed Virgin, she responded with the simple, traditional, formulaic response – 'I do!' And so, Father O'Leary, standing tall in his priestly garb, in the name of God, pronounced them man and wife.

The woodland echoed with the strains of 'Faith of our Fathers'. Shamus, the neighbouring farmer, sawed enthusiastically at his fiddle. Singing lustily in the Irish way, the guests finished with 'Here comes the bride', as newly weds Andrew and Mary wended their way between the thistles, elms and staid old oaks. They headed towards a rickety cart drawn by one solitary borrowed draught-horse. Off they clip-clopped to the allotted clearing. Then it was party time – singing and dancing and chiacking and imbibing a mysterious home-brew concocted by good neighbour Patrick O'Flaherty.

Andrew and Mary spent their first night in the bothy, enthusiastically doing what newly-weds do on that first magic night.

And, as you do if you're a carpenter with a functional hammer, a well-honed chisel and a saw that you sharpen daily, Andrew has introduced improvements to that first primitive bothy. They now have a table, two chairs, a cupboard with three shelves, two wooden bowls and a couple of clay pots. And, prompted by the optimism typical of newly-weds, a carefully crafted cradle. They now have an adequately appointed abode ... and an address! Andrew and Mary O'Laughlan – Colligan River, Dungarvan, south-east of Ireland. County Waterford.

Today, working in a clearing beside their Colligan bothy, in pleasant summery conditions, Andrew is cobbling up a table for his mate, Shamus. The job should be worth sixpence for the family coffers. The saw is blunt, the triangular file is worn, but his chisel works a treat. Instinct takes over. Andrew has a stone that he uses for the basic thirty-five degree grinding angle, followed by the finely honed twenty-five degree cutting edge. To a certain degree, it is 'guess and by golly'. But well taught by his carpenter dad, Andrew instinctively knows how to get the angles right. He can sharpen a chisel with his eyes shut. He strops it on the palm of his hand and tests it on the hairs of his left arm. He now has a three-quarter inch square bald patch just above his wrist. Yea! It's spot-on!

Forty hours' work, and a carefully crafted rustic kitchen table emerges. Andrew is happy with the finished product. Shamus, the recipient of a chunky, functional kitchen table, will be happy. And Mary will be ecstatic. There'll be food on the table – bread and dripping, boiled rabbit and ten enormous lumpers, as they called their big Irish spuds.

November, December and January of 1823 were characterised by typical Colligan meteorological conditions – bone-freezing frigidity. The two-pound question was – how do you stay warm in a bothy? It begins with the small, cuddly nature of its construction – thick walls, made of blocks of turf, an equally thick thatched roof of reeds, no windows, and a door that opens and shuts. Inside, you add a cow and two sheep, four chooks and a dog, to generate heat and at the same time provide milk, once-a-year meat, wool, fertiliser, companionship and protection from marauders. To top it off, you add a peat fire in the middle of the bothy and a small hole in the thatched roof to allow the smoke to escape. That's how you survive the icy chill and the continuous rain of a Colligan winter.

Mary has a smile on her face. In fact, she has that special mother-to-be look about her. There is an incipient bulge beneath her threadbare tunic. After a busy day 'on the tools', working for Shamus O'Donohue in Dungarvan, Andrew is home again. He shakes off the snow, takes off his mud-encrusted boots and bursts through the door with an enthusiastic greeting.

'I'm home, darling!' He engulfs her in a possessive bear-hug and smiles benignly. Then it's: 'And how's the bub?'

And her response: 'I'm going to need a new tunic!'

Together they wolf down the familiar repast of bread, spuds and bunny rabbit. Andrew had caught the rabbit the night before in a snare he'd devised – a string lasso cunningly hidden in the blackberry bushes. It goes without saying that it was last season's blackberries for dessert – cooked, preserved and frozen outside in Andrew's makeshift icebox. What gastronomic luxury! Mary undoes one more button on her tunic.

Four months later, in the month of May 1825, with a little encouragement from the local midwife, out pops a squawking, squirming babe – as it happens, a little female of the species, Brigid – 'the exalted one'. Brigid survives well on mother's milk and pratas (another Irish version for potatoes, taters, spuds or lumpers). By fifteen months she has morphed into toddler status, exploring puddles for tadpoles and the long grass for beetles and slaters, and screaming at the sight of hairy-legged spiders.

Andrew and Mary, following the Irish tradition of enthusiastically populating the earth, have made their first contribution to the eight million human beings who were to populate Ireland by the 1840s. The

Emerald Isle is splitting at the seams. Official statistics tell us that between 1820 and 1841 Ireland's population almost doubled. Subsequent events will show that the mantra, 'Populate or perish' will become 'Populate AND perish.'

Be that as it may, Andrew and Mary seem bent on making a contribution to the burgeoning statistics. Over the next seven years, four more little ones are to survive the rigours of childbirth to make the ultimate happy throng of seven.

It is September 1825. Mary is expecting again. The telltale bulge signals the arrival of a playmate for little Brigid. In the words of Henry Kendall, 'Grey Winter has gone like a wearisome guest'. And again in Henry's words, 'Behold, for repayment' is the much-desired arrival of a boy-child, Eamon. Andrew is thrilled to know that this newborn male of the species, like his father and grandfather before him, will assuredly be a potential wielder of hammer and saw.

Despite three being a crowd, it is obviously a crowd that Andrew and Mary yearn for. September 1828 marks the arrival of number three – another boy, to whom they append the traditional Irish name of Brendan – meaning 'king'. It is Mary's turn to choose the name. Despite the royal title, Brendan will probably follow the family tradition of carpentry. King of Ireland isn't an option.

Deirdre, number four, is born in the depths of winter – January 1830. She yawls with gay abandon upon being assaulted by the cold night air of a Dungarvan winter. The little hair she has is touched by a reddish tinge. She was to be the feisty one.

And finally, in February 1832, our *pièce de résistance*, Catherine, graces the scene. Catherine is the archetypal survivor. She's a scrawny, sickly little babe, but she's a fighter. It's a miracle that she survived that icy cold winter in the Colligan hills. Mother's milk and lots of love from her parents and siblings gave her adequate reason to fight the odds and win.

Despite her small body mass, Mary was able to generate enough life-sustaining milk to set Catherine on the path to good health. At a time when a third of newborns in hospitals did not survive their first year, all too often babies born in the bush were able to beat these statistics. This was an era when a staid and stubborn medical fraternity did not understand the cause of infection. Often babies born in the countryside, away from disease-infected, unwashed hands of so-called doctors who had just completed an autopsy, had a better chance of survival.

As subsequent events prove, Catherine was indeed a survivor.

The cold of winter in the Colligan Hills had its own risks. In the stifling, smoky confines of Andrew and Mary's crowded bothy, they relied on one smouldering peat fire in the middle of the room. Smoke spiralled up though the hole in the thatched roof. The calorific output of this fire was supplemented by the body heat generated by the seven human bodies, one cow, two sheep, four chooks, Blue – the reddish-brown mongrel dog – and the tabby cat of unknown progeny. The cramped conditions of the bothy were an advantage when it came to conserving heat and staying warm in a savage Irish winter.

On a typical night, the bothy reverberated with the colicky screams of a new-born babe, not to mention squeals of excitement from Eamon and Brendan over two frogs they'd captured the day before, that jumped around the bothy, and four-year-old Brigid singing 'Faith of our Fathers' loudly and with conviction, and little Deidre screaming ear-piercingly for her turn at mother's milk. It was utter mayhem!

Andrew was about to lose his customary cool.

'Shut up, you lot! I've had a hard day on the tools and I'm completely wrecked. Why did I ever choose to have kids?' He looks at Mary. 'Ah yeah! I remember now!' He ruminates for a moment, but can't resist a minor whinge. 'Twelve hours straight and a crook back! It's bleedin' hard work, to say the least.'

No wonder he's tetchy! It takes the calm, cool, insistent 'Shhhhhh' from Mary to finally settle them down. 'OK, Andy and kids, it's time for the rosary!'

There is a chorus of muted 'Ohhhhhs'.

'Then we can have our yummy badger soup. And as many pratas as you can eat. And crab apples for dessert.'

More 'Ohhhhhhhhhs', this time with a rising inflection. 'Yum-meeeee!'

The Blight

Everything went well till the potatoes began to turn black and rotten in the ground. The first signs were in 1845.

Andrew and Mary and their offspring survived the first year despite the initial impact of the blight. Their potatoes were not as yet affected. But in the subsequent year, 1846, the blight began to proliferate. The rot, so to speak, had really set in. It made its way inexorably up to the Colligan Hills. Prospective furniture buyers were now few and far between. Chairs and tables were a luxury that the locals could ill afford. They chose to sit on the ground to partake of their meagre fare. Without work, Andrew could no longer pay the rent. His potato crop turned black and putrid – no income, no food on the table. The landlord from his English mansion became impatient. He was no longer the friendly landlord.

Andrew sold his family table and chairs for a pittance. By 1847 it was all over. The family were evicted. They headed for the hills. High on the barren mountain, Andrew set up a lean-to on land that no landlord wanted. The blight followed them and proceeded to destroy them systematically. With no work, no food, no bothy, they all fell ill. Without their life-sustaining potatoes, weak and hungry, the children were the first to fall victim of malnourishment and disease. Andrew and Mary went without food to feed the children with whatever they could scrounge. It was to no avail.

It was the same story everywhere for the predominately Catholic population of Ireland. Country folk, in particular, were systematically targeted by an array of potentially fatal illnesses – tuberculosis, measles, cholera, typhus, smallpox, dysentery – not to mention starvation. The children could not cope with the onslaught of disease and hunger as well as the average adult. Four of Andrew and Mary's children – Brigid, Eamon, Brendan and Deirdre – succumbed to a combination of the above and died within the year. Catherine, despite her frail constitution, survived.

Unable to pay their debts, incapable of surviving in the barren hills above Dungarvan, and on the brink of despair, Andrew and Mary accepted the humiliating option of the Dungarvan Workhouse. Catherine, now fifteen years of age, joined her parents there.

In return for two meals a day – a bowl of watery swill, a plate of Indian corn and a portion of bread – they were expected to work ten gruelling hours. As a result of exposure to the elements and starvation, both parents were in an appalling physical condition. Starvation, weight loss, exposure to the elements and any number of diseases had taken their toll.

Gibson, in his study of the Irish workhouse, writes:

*Medical care almost everywhere was scant and reluctantly
granted. Workhouse patients commonly underwent surgery
without anaesthetics to keep down the costs. Disease was endemic.
Tuberculosis of two types – phthisis (or consumption) and scrofula,
which affected bones, muscle and skin, were notoriously rife –
and typhus was a constant fear. Measles killed more children in*

*the nineteenth century than any other illness. Whooping cough
and croup killed tens of thousands more, and no place was more
conducive to their spread than a stale and crowded workhouse.*

Dietary insufficiencies made threadworms and tapeworms more or less
universal. A patent medicine company in Manchester produced 'a pur-
gative which was guaranteed to expel, faithfully and perhaps explosively, every unwelcome parasite in the intestinal tract.' One user proudly
testified that he had brought forth three hundred worms, some of them
'of uncommon thickness'.

It was indeed 'survival of the fittest' and more by good luck than
good management. In modern times, illnesses such as measles, whooping cough and tuberculosis are minor blips in our lives given the avail-
ability of modern medicines such as penicillin.

By 1848 there were 2781 inmates in the Dungarvan workhouse. At
the same time, outside the workhouse, the dispossessed, the debt-ridden
and the hungry joined forces in the Dungarvan Riots. They stormed and
looted the warehouse on the Dungarvan Quay. Forces of law and order
intervened and the riot was quickly suppressed. But brute force did not
solve the hunger problem of a desperate population.

Meanwhile, within the workhouse, Andrew, weakened by disease,
was entrusted with the challenging task of digging drains. He was a
mere vestige of his former self, reduced to skin and bone and plagued
by the debilitating effects of typhus and cholera. He could barely wield
the pickaxe and shovel, the preferred workhouse digging implements.
Four weeks later, weak and racked by disease, Andrew collapsed into
the drain he was digging. The overseer, taken aback by Andrew's dramatic fall and disappointed by his meagre work output, committed him
to the Dungarvan Fever Hospital.

Mary, in the women's quarters, fared no better. Ten hours a day
scrubbing floors and pummelling linen in giant vats was more than her

disease-ridden body could bear. Physically debilitated, she likewise succumbed, collapsing in a faint beside a tub of soaking sheets, towels and underwear. She was likewise committed to the Fever Hospital.

By the middle of 1848, Andrew and Mary were both at death's door. They died within two weeks of each other, leaving fifteen-year-old Catherine totally distraught and abandoned. She was truly now the archetypal Irish Potato Famine orphan.

Andrew and Mary were buried in the Pulla Cemetery close to Dungarvan in what was commonly known as the old Slievegrine Graveyard. Famine victims were interred *en masse*, in unmarked graves. Separated by death, Andrew and Mary made their final journey by a horse and cart uphill to the Slievegrine Graveyard.

The poem, '*Na Prátai Dubha*' ('The Black Potatoes') by Máire Ní Dhroma graphically tells this story of a mass tragic loss of life and the misery of those left behind:

> *Poor children shouting that scream,*
> *Poorhouse bolted and cold.*
> *Married couples separated in death,*
> *Famished waifs tasting the soup of misery.*

Death was followed by immediate burial in those days, for obvious reasons. Catherine sobbed helplessly and hopelessly at the burial sites of each parent.

Despite the company of hundreds of fellow victims of the Irish Potato Famine, Catherine felt like a lost soul. She missed her family and fell into deep depression. She wanted to die like the rest of her family. But suddenly her God intervened and the O'Laughlan resilience kicked in. She woke up one morning and set her mind to the task of turning around her negative mind-set, bravely and uncompromisingly declaring through gritted teeth: 'I am the sole survivor of the O'Laughlan family. I owe it to them to keep their memory alive. So go to it, girl! Get cracking! Think positively. Survive. Find yourself a man. Bring more kids into the world, and carry on the O'Laughlan family spirit.'

The presence of so many other orphans in a similar plight stirred in her some hope for the future. She had much to learn about life and the world. Chatting with her new-found workhouse companions, Catherine learnt about the world beyond Dungarvan. The sad fact was that Catherine was illiterate. She couldn't even spell her own name. Nevertheless, in practical matters, she was a quick learner, more interested in acquiring manual skills like plaiting, spinning and weaving than manipulating quills dipped in ink to generate mysterious symbols. She never learned to read or write. Signing documents meant placing her own special brand of X at the end of whatever document she was asked to sign. Catherine's version of X was more akin to a plus sign, as birth certificates, baptism registers and hospital documentation attest in later years. Literacy was not a priority.

In the weeks to come, Catherine's first job was the soul-destroying task of unplaiting coarse ships' hawsers impregnated with pitch. Having separated the prickly sisal fibres, with hands red-raw and lacerated by constant contact with old anchor and mainsail ropes, she scraped away the pitch and then stacked the fibres for dispatch to the rope-maker. Hawser-work was one of her least favourite duties.

Soon she was to graduate to the kitchen, where she worked from dawn to dusk washing and scrubbing pots and pans. Chatting was actively discouraged. Nevertheless, despite the clatter of kitchenware and the splashing of water, Catherine managed to sneak in a word here and there with the other girl-orphans and in the process made a few good friends. Whenever the supervisor left the room, they chatted surreptitiously about the prospects of ultimately escaping the confines of the workhouse.

Just when she had got used to dish-washing, Catherine was moved to laundry duties, which meant relentless washing, scrubbing and wringing out in ice cold water an endless pile of soiled orphan clothing. This formidable stack of malodorous, faded linen seemed to grow rather than diminish, no matter how hard she washed and scrubbed.

When the weather was fine enough, the laundry girls hung the washing to dry on the clothesline behind the workhouse. Catherine loved nothing more than to watch the shirts, socks, undies and skirts ballooning and dancing in the wind. And she and her mates cheered when the line balancing on a ten-foot clothes prop swung from one side to the other. Simple pleasures are all too often the best.

After a pleasant enough three months in the laundry, Catherine was promoted. She was finally entrusted to the *crème de la crème* – the spinning wheel. Now she was able to treadle away blissfully, hour after relaxing hour. Spinning yarn and reconstituting old wool and flax ready for the weavers in the next room was a pleasantly mindless way of spending her ten-hour work day. Life in the workhouse was definitely better than the alternative.

At the end of a long day, after a meagre meal of bread, Indian meal and thin gruel, Catherine lay on her hard bunk dreaming about the 'great southern land' – the faraway country called Australia that her orphan mates talked about. Her concept of geography and her sense of space were limited. They told her Australia was at the other end of the world, whatever that meant. The other girls constantly chatted about the Australian dream – sunshine, gold, kangaroos and wide-open spaces and plenty of food including good, healthy disease-free potatoes. It sounded like heaven on earth. Year after year, boatloads of girl-orphans from the ages of fifteen to twenty were sent off to Australia. Catherine's dream was to join them.

Catherine's time in the workhouse was not all beer and skittles. There were quite a few challenging, defining moments when her resilience was severely tested. On the one hand, there were the managers and matrons who demanded discipline and obedience to the plethora of restricting rules to which inmates were expected to adhere. On the other hand, as well as the impoverished but well-intentioned young girls, there were the difficult, undisciplined, self-centred, thieving, lying inmates that you inevitably come across in all kinds of institutions.

There was one defining incident that tested Catherine to the limit. She had managed to hang on to a few personal possessions apart from a box of well-worn clothing. They included a few treasured knick-knacks that had survived the tented existence in the mountains. There was one special item that Catherine guarded with her life. It was a little wooden doll, ten inches high, carved by her father.

Topsy had a curly mop of sheep's wool hair, two beady eyes, a button nose and a mouth that opened and closed. She had arms that swivelled outwards in a fond embrace, and legs that articulated at the waist and knees. She could stand, sit, kneel and reach out to her owner. As a little girl, Catherine attached strings to the crown of Topsy's head, knees and wrists, so that she could now walk, run, dance, nod, bow and wave to her owner. Topsy was Catherine's most treasured possession and a constant reminder of her clever and loving dad Andrew.

One day, two months into her term in the Dungarvan workhouse, in accordance with her daily routine, Catherine checked under her paltry stash of clothes to bid 'Good morning!' to little Topsy. Topsy had vanished. Devastated, Catherine churned over her options. Should she discuss her problem with the supervisor, the matron, the nurse or her orphan friends? No! She had to investigate herself – now – while the trail was hot.

Cathy trusted no one but herself. She waited till all had set off for their daily duties. She loitered in the bunkroom till the coast was clear. She hesitated about prying into other girls' meagre possessions, but the stakes were high. She was aware of three others with suspect reputations – the light-fingered types. So Cathy decided to bend the rules and investigate – surreptitiously.

Her first suspect was Meg McConachy. Cathy made a beeline for Meg's bunk and the flimsy box underneath. She quickly rifled through Meg's scant possessions – dirty clothes and underwear mainly. No Topsy!

The next possibility was Susie Sweeney. Same scenario. Susie displayed higher standards of both hygiene and tidiness. Same result! Nothing!

This left her with her final suspect – Abigail O'Flaherty. The mystery suddenly unravelled. Under a tangle of holed black socks, a bluish top, a faded brown dress and two pairs of moth-eaten undies of uncertain colour, there she was – Topsy!

Work finished at seven o'clock that night. After the evening meal, the exhausted inmates retired to the dormitory. Matron, in the next room, left the girls to their own devices, assuming that all were ready for sleep after their hard ten hours' work. But Cathy, unlike the others, was not asleep. Matron was snoring in her adjoining bedroom. Cathy crept over to Abigail O'Flaherty's top-storey bunk and dug her in the ribs. Abigail woke with a start.

In a loud whisper, Cathy challenged her about the theft. Abigail leapt down from her bunk, and being quite adept in dealing with confrontation, seized a handful of Cathy's hair, knocking her to the floor and pummelling her with her closed left fist. Apparently Abigail had long since learnt that the best form of defence is attack. Cathy, who had learnt a few tricks of her own from scuffling with her brothers, rolled over and reciprocated by entwining her fingers into Abigail's copious knotted tresses. It was a battle of wills. They used their left hands for scratching, pinching and pummelling. Screaming was not an option. They knew that Matron was a light sleeper. But the others, excited by the noise of the scuffle, jumped from their bunks and began to cheer – in muted whispers!

But Matron in the next room hears all. In she burst and the culprits were in serious trouble. They spent the rest of the night standing in the corner of Matron's room. The following day they were tried, judged, condemned and subjected to an appropriate punishment – three days in solitary on bread and water. To Cathy it was a triumph. The three days went quickly – no work and a much-needed rest. A win-win situation! Topsy was greeted with respect from all. Cathy was treated with universal acclaim.

The one hundred and fifty workhouses in Ireland were bursting at the seams. A million Irish Catholics would ultimately die during the Potato Famine. Another million were to migrate to America, Canada, New Zealand and Australia. There was excitement in the air.

Between 1846 and '51, nineteen ships laden with Potato Famine orphan girls were to take to the seas, destination Australia. You had to be between fifteen and twenty, single and an orphan to qualify. The word was out. Cathy and her friends were excited, apprehensive and bewildered by the prospect of leaving the Ireland they knew and loved. The worn-out cliché about 'nothing ventured, nothing gained' was particularly pertinent. Their future in Ireland was pretty bleak. The possibility of a new life in a new country, masses of sunshine, a well-paid job and a well-off husband was a prospect not to be sneezed at. When the chance happened, they jumped at it.

It was a numbers game. Let's look at the stats. Matron was faced with the unenviable task of choosing 110 healthy, hard-working orphan-girls. By the middle of 1849, there were 2223 inmates in the Dungarvan Workhouse; 654 of these were female orphans between the ages of fifteen and twenty, and who therefore qualified for a new life in far-away Australia. To be chosen, you had to be adaptable, honest, clean, and above all, you had to have 'the right attitude'.

The *New Liverpool* was almost ready to sail. Of the twenty ships bound for Australia, we have records from five, including the *New*

Liverpool. Some ships, crammed to the gills, took as many as 300 orphans. The *New Liverpool* already had approximately sixty paying passengers. Shipping records from 1849 show that *New Liverpool's* master, Captain Horace Boldrewood, was prepared to take 240 female orphans at a cost of six pounds per orphan. The more he crammed into his ship, the more for his already bulging pockets.

The cost of transporting the orphans was to be borne by the Colonial Government and the Crown. The Colonial Government had raised funds by selling crown land and were quite able to make their contribution. Many of the well-to-do Protestants objected to such funds being wasted on Irish Catholic orphans. But Australia needed young females who were hard-working and prepared to pair up with the thousands of male settlers without partners, particularly gold-miners. Therefore the Crown and the new colony were prepared to divide the costs between them.

Choosing potential candidates with the right attitude was paramount. Matron had her reputation to consider. Two basic conditions were demanded – the potential to work hard, and the will to take on the harsh colonial life of the antipodes.

Catherine, the 'brawling wild-cat' was not chosen. At the last minute Maisie McAlpin fell ill with pneumonia. A replacement was needed. Matron looked over the remaining 415 sad-eyed orphans. It was then that she noticed skinny little Catherine forlornly clutching her little wooden puppet-doll. She had previously dismissed Catherine as a troublemaker. Matron pondered for a moment and then said to herself:

'Hmmm! How about Catherine O'Laughlan, the feisty little blue-eyed poppet. She might just be the one to survive that harsh three-month trip. She's a gutsy one. Maybe we'll give her another chance. I really believe she's got what it takes to make good in a rough, tough Australia.' Matron pointed her long bony finger at Catherine. 'Off you go, girl, and don't let me down!'

Catherine jumped to her feet, grabbed her meagre possessions, and joined the other one hundred and nine who had already gathered around the workhouse entrance with their meagre possessions.

Catherine's inclusion amongst the successful Dungarvan candidates is verified in the official 'Public Records Office Archives of Victoria', the only anomaly being the creative spelling of her name. She is listed as Loughlin, Catherine, this being one of six versions we meet in a variety of records – O'Loughlan, McLaughlan, O'Loughlin, O'Laughlin, O'Laughlan, the last of which is the most frequently used in public documents. Catherine herself stubbornly continued to sign official documents with an X, thus avoiding the issue of how to spell her name.

High Seas to Australia

One hundred and ten Dungarvan Workhouse girl orphans marched down towards the Docks. Matron tried in vain to control the excited chatter. With the assistance of three other attendants she managed to keep them in pairs as the straggling line of orphans snaked its way towards the little steamboat. As they turned a bend in the road, it was then that they saw it: a small vessel in the harbour below belching smoke into the sky as it sat obediently at the wharf. It was indeed just like John Masefield's 'dirty British coaster with salt-caked smoke-stack'. The little ship's capacity was one hundred and fifty. It was bursting at the seams. The girls had to crowd on to the deck shoulder to shoulder, clutching their meagre possessions. With a shrill shriek from its ear-piercing whistle, the little steamer began to make its tentative way from the shallow Dungarvan harbour to the open sea.

The orphans crammed on to the deck clutched each other in trepidation and excitement. The ship was finally under way, puffing under its load. Buffeted by the waves, they headed bravely towards the south-east, destination Liverpool. What could possibly go wrong?

Then began three horrific days of torture, of alternately standing, crouching, and lying on the wooden planks between a tangle of arms and legs. They hugged each other in the cold as the little steamer relentlessly fought the wild seas between Dungarvan and Portsmouth. The little craft shuddered, rocked and rolled, and all too often waves broke over the deck, drenching the shivering girls. Together with the physical buffeting, there was the constant roar of the waves and the desperate moans of their friends. Although they were used to physical challenges, this was something quite different again. They wallowed in vomit that swilled over the deck, to be washed away by the drenching waves. Catherine like the others, as the uncouth amongst us would say, 'coughed her guts out'. Fortunately, bad things, like good things, usually come to an end.

Suddenly it was Portsmouth on the portside. They had survived a horrific ordeal. That's what they were by definition – *survivors*.

A half-mile ahead the bosun pointed out a tall three-masted sailing ship – the *New Liverpool*. This was to be their home for the next hundred or so days. No more cramped conditions on deck exposed to wind, rain and brain-numbing cold. They were now excitedly looking forward to the comparative comfort of this graceful 'monarch of the sea', as the bosun called it.

The steamboat nudged its way between numerous other craft, large and small, and landed at the dock adjacent to the *New Liverpool*. With a communal sigh of relief they were allowed to put their feet once again on *terra firma* while the passengers below deck disembarked. A few minutes later they were climbing up the gangplank of this mighty barque.

Catherine and her newfound friends, Beth, Shaelah and Siobhan, had the impression that travelling halfway round the world in a graceful sailing ship was the stuff of longed-for dreams. Their elation was somewhat dimmed as they were directed deep into the malodorous bowels of the ship, to what was called the steerage. The upper deck had already been taken by the fee-paying passengers. The middle deck was assigned to the Waterford Workhouse contingent together with half the girls from Cork.

As the late arrivals, Cathy and her fellow inmates were assigned to steerage, where they joined the balance of the Cork orphans. The 'Corkers', as they called them, had already taken the best bunks. Conditions were crowded but tolerable. They were surrounded by cables and levers, which they were informed were used to steer the ship. The middle and steerage decks had to accommodate 240 girls in all. The paying passengers were able to afford the comparative 'luxury' of the top deck.

In general, this disparate group of young females, a mix of the more promising inmates from the Cork, Dungarvan and Waterford workhouses, got on well together. They were grateful for the chance of a new life in a faraway land and thought positively about the future. There were the inevitable minor conflicts, but in general most behaved themselves.

Passing steamers caused their ship to rock gently in the swell. Being in steerage, their ears were assailed by the ominous creaking of timbers and the sound of sloshing water in the bilges below. Their noses were distinctly aware of the malodorous admixture of various human excretions. The good thing about the olfactory function of noses is that they soon get used to surrounding odours, pleasant and otherwise.

It was comforting to know that the six-foot-high ceiling would protect them from the elements. The wooden bunks, one above the other and with straw palliasses, were designed to accommodate five persons of average dimensions side by side. Such sleeping arrangements looked so inviting after the standing room only trip from Dungarvan to Portsmouth. Each bunk was supplied with two communal blankets to enable them to deal with the variety of climatic conditions they would meet during the journey, from the moderate coolness of a British summer to the frigid conditions of the Southern Ocean. Of course it would be blanket-doffing time when they reached the stifling heat of the Equator.

Discipline was strict. The girls were not permitted to wander up to the deck for that longed-for breath of fresh air. But, providing the hatches were open, breathing, despite the putrid nature of the stale air, was not a serious problem. They were warned that it was only when a storm blew up and the seas were tumultuous that the order would be given to batten down the hatches. Then the air would become stifling, and the below-deck inmates would be left gasping for breath.

Over the years, scurvy had been a serious problem, particularly on long journeys. But Captain Cook's enlightened view on the necessity of fresh juice and vegetables had largely solved the problem. Cabbage was quite effective. It was cheap, and it lasted well between stopovers. Fortunately, there would be no cases of scurvy during Catherine's trip to Australia.

Three days later, sails were unfurled amidst the barking of orders, the screeching of winches, and the releasing of hawsers, to the cries of 'Anchors aweigh!' The sails ballooned as they crept tentatively out of the harbour, negotiating their way between craft of all shapes and sizes. At last they were in the open sea. They rocked and wallowed as they battled their way against a blustering easterly, which pummelled them from the direction of the English Channel.

Most of the girls, including Catherine, had more or less developed their sea legs during the trip from Ireland. But there were still those who vomited with gay abandon – relentlessly and copiously. Amongst the latter was Catherine's best friend Siobhan, who had serious intestinal issues. Her other good friends, Beth and Shaelah, had by now developed the same resistant constitution as Catherine. Soon we have our one hundred and ten Dungarvan orphan girls, not to mention the Cork lot, sloshing round in puddles of vomit, which eventually finished up in the bilges, leaving behind that all-pervasive 'vomituous' [our son Simon's little boy version of *vomitous*] odour that inexorably hangs in the air. They were eventually given five buckets of seawater with which to sluice down the steerage deck.

According to the 1849 *New Liverpool* passenger manifest, there was a staff of five to attend to the needs of two hundred and forty girls. Leading the team was head matron Mary Anne Murray, who was assisted by sub-matron Susan Burton. It was an impossible and quite overwhelming task, but they did their best. Their best meant providing food, clean drinking water, basic health solutions, catering for the specific needs of young women, overseeing waste disposal, and ensuring adherence to ship-board rules.

The support team included two young, inexperienced teachers, Catherine Canning and Catherine Grainger. The two Catherines tried their best to instil basic reading and writing skills into these largely unreceptive orphan girls. Most of them had never been to school and were totally illiterate. The two Catherines rarely made it down to the lower deck where our Catherine and her friends were installed.

Before their incarceration in the workhouse, a handful of the more fortunate of the orphan girls had had the questionable advantage of a day here and there attending illegal 'hedge schools' taught by itinerant teachers. These hedge schools were strictly forbidden by the English authorities. Hence the chance of basic literacy skills was limited to very few children from Catholic potato-farming families.

On a few occasions, our two young teachers visited the steerage deck. Despite their best intentions, these aspiring pedagogues made little impact on Catherine and her friends. Catherine O'Laughlan, although quite intelligent in her own way, continued to be stubbornly illiterate for the rest of her days.

The fifth person in the team of five was Eliza Quin, the needle-woman. Eliza made it her personal mission to access the girls on the lower deck, whom she saw as most in need of her attention. Catherine had always been interested in stitching and couldn't resist showing Eliza her most treasured possession – Topsy, the doll-puppet. Eliza was fascinated. Because of the proliferation of Catherines on board, she decided to call her Cathy. The name stuck. While Cathy never learnt to read and write, she became quite an accomplished plier of needle and thread. Her specialty was repairing torn and worn-out garments – everything from hose, dresses and coats to threadbare underwear.

The team of five meant well, working hard from dawn till dusk, and they had reason to be proud of their record during this voyage. The fact that there was only one death on this long and hazardous journey is a testament to their dedication and efficiency.

Within a day or two, most of the girls had acclimatised to the motion of the ship as it ploughed its way southwards towards their first stopover – Lisbon. The food, though basic, satisfied the cravings of their empty stomachs. They were served such culinary delights as oatmeal porridge for breakfast, a generous soupy swill for lunch, and a chunk of salted beef with cabbage and rock-hard bread for dinner. These hungry orphan girls were in heaven. Catherine and her friends, Shaelah and Beth, ate ravenously of each humble repast. But all too often Siobhan's delicate constitution could not cope with rich food in such generous quantities. She chucked up – in style!

A downside to life below deck was having to share their quarters with a multitude of rats, fleas and cockroaches. The rats emerged boldly at night, searching for crumbs and whatever scum they could find in unwashed bowls. These cheeky rodents even nibbled the toes of their sleeping victims who, if they woke, would kick and scream. If they were quick, they might grab the odd rat by the tail and squash its bewhiskered head against the side of the bunk. These and other creatures invaded every crevice and cranny in the crowded confines of steerage accommodation. Fleas were as bad as the rats because they were so relentless. They attacked the most private parts of these young girls. Catherine and her friends competed with each other as they tried to catch and crush these supremely gymnastic acrobats that jumped from victim to victim. They scratched and slapped from morning to night. As for the roaches, with their distinctive odour and tough, impact-resisting carapace, they scurried back and forth looking for a place to hide. The challenge was to crush them with a shoe before they made it to safety. Cockroaches revelled in the general state of uncleanliness below deck. They competed with the rats as the most hated of all these predators.

Bathing facilities were non-existent. Many spent the whole 107 days unwashed and malodorous. Catherine, Shaelah, Siobhan and Beth, who were known as the cleanliness freaks, availed themselves of the occasional bucket of cold seawater. Siobhan's delicate constitution was seriously challenged by offensive odours and the generally unsanitary conditions on board this 1849 long-haul sailing ship. Periodically, the crew manually operated pumps to remove bilge water, which constantly leaked through the aging timbers below the steerage deck. Plumbing was basic and primitive. Human-generated products, like sewage, vomit, menstruation solutions and general waste disposal depended on buckets. Their contents were ritually disposed of overboard. The ubiquitous bucket solved so many problems. It was the source of drinking water, water for ablutions, as well as a means of disposing of human excretions. Fortunately a different bucket was used for each purpose.

New Liverpool was making good progress. Suddenly the girls heard the loud cry from the coxswain: 'Lisbon ahead – portside!.' The crew on the upper deck cheered. The well-heeled passengers on the quarterdeck took up the cry. The orphan girls from the bowels of the ship with their shrill soprano voices followed suit. Captain Horace Boldrewood smiled his enigmatic smile.

They landed. They replenished supplies. They filled their tanks with fresh clean water. It was fresh fruit for all. They chanted, 'Oranges and lemons, the bells of St Clement's.' And ever so quickly they were again on the way south, heading towards the Roaring Forties they'd heard so much about.

One month later, *New Liverpool* sat motionless on a silent flat sea. No Roaring Forties – yet! They were on the Equator. Totally becalmed. The sun blazed down relentlessly. The heat was enervating and stultifying. The sails hung listlessly. *New Liverpool* sat helplessly under an unforgiving sun. The sailors lolled about in a dream. Below deck was an oven. One compassionate sailor handed out to the sweltering orphans buckets of seawater with which to cool their overheated bodies. Drinking water was rationed. Just enough to survive!

The Ancient Mariner, in the classic poem by Samuel Taylor Coleridge, summed it up perfectly:

> *Day after day, day after day,*
> *We stuck, nor breath, nor motion;*
> *As idle as a painted ship*
> *Upon a painted ocean.*

Ten sultry, suffocating days later, the sails began to stir. Ever so gradually they resumed their path southwards, destination Cape Town. Water was still severely rationed. Their throats were parched. Severely dehydrated, they tried to raise a cheer. At least they were on the move again.

Then the miracle they were praying for happened. The wind picked up in earnest. The ship's master gave the welcome order to ease water restrictions. The longed-for wind had finally kicked in. The sails thumped and then billowed. They took off towards the south in style. Two weeks later they were at Cape Town.

Cape Town meant replenishment of depleted water supplies, fresh fruit – particularly the scurvy-fighting citrus, a generous restocking of cabbage, and a top-up of salted beef. The wind was now blowing a gale outside the harbour. Forty knots on the open sea. There was a job to be done – and quickly. It was a question of all hands on deck – all sixty of them. This meant that every able-bodied crewmember, from Captain Boldrewood, officers, boatswain, mate, riggers, swabbers, sail-makers, down to the cook and the humblest bottle-washer, had to play their part in quickly restocking the ship. One and all, they formed a human chain and were totally focused on the task of ferrying supplies to the ship and stowing them as quickly as possible. The wind waits for no one!

Meanwhile, all passengers, orphans included, were given an hour in which to stretch their legs and breathe deeply of the fresh salt air. For sixty precious minutes, Catherine, Shaelah, Siobhan and Beth were deliciously engulfed by the blinding sunshine and enraptured by the vibrant blue sky. Siobhan was feeling better. Delivered temporally from the foul odours of polluted bilge water and human excreta, they luxuriated in the invigorating freshness of the untainted sea air. But this respite was all too short-lived.

The penetrating blast of the foghorn brought them back to reality. Return to quarters immediately! The replenishment of supplies had been completed in record time. There was a strong favourable wind on the starboard bow. From below deck they could hear the booming voice of the ship's master. Then whistles and shouts from the crew. Anchors aweigh. A rattle of chains. The flapping of sails. All trim, taut and ready to go! And *New Liverpool* edged out of the harbour, destination Melbourne Town.

If they were lucky, they could do the final run from the Cape of Good Hope to Melbourne within six weeks. They had supplies for eight weeks. *New Liverpool* was well stocked for what can only be described as a final roller-coaster journey through some of the most challenging waters of the Southern Ocean. They waved goodbye to the Cape of Good Hope with their hearts full of optimistic good hope for this last stage.

New Liverpool rounded the Cape in style and headed towards the Roaring Forties. Captain and crew had to keep a close lookout for stray ice floes as they edged southwards. Many a ship went down, *Titanic*-style, looking for a quicker run, tempted by the diminishing circumference of the earth and the strong prevailing winds of the Roaring Forties.

The seas became more erratic and the waves more mountainous. Each successive wall of water, eighty feet high, towered above them from the depths of each successive trough. Catherine and her friends, confined as they were to steerage, did not see these massive walls of water that threatened to engulf their tiny barque. But they certainly felt them. They experienced the unnerving sensation of leaving their stomachs and sometimes their contents behind with each dramatic plunge. But somehow the good ship *New Liverpool* managed to climb the face of each mountainous wall of water. They teetered on the peak before plunging down the face of the next succeeding wave.

All moveable objects were tied down. Untethered tables and chairs were stacked away. The sea and the wind roared ominously around them. The weather was now bitterly cold in stark contrast to the suffocating heat of the Doldrums.

Siobhan's physical condition had taken a turn for the worse. She coughed and shivered constantly and experienced severe, debilitating weakness, coupled with gut-wrenching nausea. The ship's surgeon diagnosed a severe case of pneumonia. Cathy, Beth and Shaelah attended to her constantly. They surrendered their own blankets. They force-fed her with spoons-full of their own warm broth. But to no avail. The ship's dramatic diving into watery canyons and the bitter cold were more than her weakened constitution could bear. Spasms of uncontrollable coughing, feverish hallucinations, shortness of breath and spasmodic vomiting took their toll.

Ten days later, Siobhan gasped one final breath and then quietly departed this world. Her three friends were inconsolable. This was different to the deaths in the workhouse. Just as they were approaching their Promised Land, one of their best friends had suddenly succumbed to a disease that others were known to survive.

Siobhan's frail remains were encased in a canvas body bag and weighed down with a bar of pigiron, retrieved from the ship's precious ballast. The captain pronounced the traditional prayers before committing her lifeless body to the deep. Siobhan bumped her way to the end of the plank before plunging irrevocably into a watery grave.

The three friends clung to each other sobbing helplessly and hopelessly as they bade farewell to their friend.

The final rush from Cape Town to Melbourne was to take altogether forty-three rollicking days. They were now halfway between Cape Town and their final destination. *New Liverpool* seemed to pause momentarily on the peak of a mountainous swell. A tiny island bobbed up between the waves on the port side. The boatswain, in a loud, portentous voice, announced that they were passing the Ile Saint-Paul – the mid-point between Cape Town and Melbourne. The excited message was passed down into the bowels of the ship. The orphan girls cheered spontaneously as the significance of this little insignificant scrap of land was spread around. They were now on the home run. They continued to be driven relentlessly by the prevailing westerlies towards Melbourne.

It seemed to happen so suddenly. A dark shadow on the horizon. Landfall. The promised land! The long wild days had paid off. Two hundred and thirty-nine orphan girls, now one less after the sad loss of Siobhan, were allowed up on deck to view their final destination – AUSTRALIA. They let loose their pent-up emotions, screaming excitedly as young girls do.

No time to waste. Maybe one more week and a bit. Making the most of the strong westerlies, the captain kept an eagle eye on diminishing supplies, at the same time focusing on maps, the compass, the weather and the unpredictable seas of the Great Australian Bight.

Melbourne Town

Twelve days later, *New Liverpool* was heading towards the narrow channel leading into Port Phillip Bay. The Rip, as it was called, was subject to unpredictable, treacherous seas and tidal changes. It consisted of a narrow half-mile gap that was to herald the doom of hundreds of unwary ships. In 1849, there was a primitive system of self-appointed pilots in whaleboats rowed by convicts, directing difficult-to-manoeuvre sailing ships through the treacherous Rip. Captain Boldrewood, following directions from pilot Gerry Tobin, carefully negotiated the Rip on the incoming tide. *New Liverpool* was swept through the middle of the turbulent waters unscathed. Forty hours later, after negotiating tortuous channels, they made it to the safety of the Port of Melbourne. It was the morning of 9 August 1849. The voyage from Plymouth to Melbourne had taken a total of 107 days.

Hundreds of craft of all shapes and sizes lolled about waiting for action. *New Liverpool* inched her way towards her berth at the Port of Melbourne dock. Two hundred and thirty-nine Irish orphan girls emerged from the bowels of the ship – excited, bewildered, blinded by the dazzling sun and clutching their meagre possessions. They couldn't believe their ears when they learnt that stacked within the hold was a further generous box of supplies allocated to each orphan:

- 6 shifts, 6 pairs of stockings (2 worsted and 4 cotton), 2 pairs of shoes
- 2 gowns (one of warm material – woollen plaid), 2 short wrappers
- 2 flannel petticoats, 2 cotton petticoats, 1 shawl, 1 cloak
- 2 neck and 3 pocket-handkerchiefs, 2 linen collars, 3 aprons
- 1 pair of stays, 1 pair of sheets, 1 pair of mitts
- 1 bonnet, day and night caps, 2 towels
- 2 lb of soap, combs and brushes, needles, thread, a few yards of cotton
- Bible (Douay version) and Prayer Book for Roman Catholics
- One box for each emigrant – length 2 feet, width 14 inches, depth 14 inches, with lock and key, emigrant's name painted on the front and a catalogue of contents pasted on the inside of lid.

Why was such generous support offered for the new arrivals? Here's the answer. Costs for transporting the girls to Australia, at six pounds per orphan, were met from two sources. First, the Irish Protestant establishment wanted a cheap and efficient way of reducing burgeoning workhouse costs. Their share of three pounds per orphan was cheap at twice the price. Second, the largely Protestant establishment in Australia wanted cheap labour as well as partners for the predominantly male population of this new colony. They were quite happy to make a similar contribution, making up a total of six pounds per orphan. The orphan girl solution was a win-win situation for both parties. Furthermore, the girls needed to be independent from additional handouts from the very start. Adequate clothing was the first step in making them employable and an attractive proposition for prospective employers.

Meanwhile, Cathy and her bewildered friends staggered under their load as they made their way down the gangplank. They were surrounded by a sea of faces and battered by a barrage of insistent male voices. They were thrilled to think that they were the source of so much male attention. But it soon became clear that it was not only their feminine charms that attracted so much male interest, but just as much their potential as a source of cheap labour. Females, particularly the orphan kind, were viewed as undemanding, economical, and generally characterised by a positive work ethic. With this in mind, they would be bound as apprentices till the age of eighteen. They would then move into the category of prospective female companionship for lonely single males, as well as diligent, uncomplaining, grateful workhorses.

Suddenly Cathy was engulfed by the press of a noisy crowd. Prospective male employers prodded and poked at her and bombarded her with a myriad of questions. Although she revelled in being the centre of attention, she was acutely embarrassed by the male eyes that eyed her over as though she were a prize filly, or, worse, a young girl to be taken advantage of.

In the crowd, there was a certain portly gentleman in a top hat who was looking Catherine up and down with interest. It was Thomas Graham, sitting high on his buggy and eying the talent below with practised eye. Thomas Graham had many fingers in many pies, and, at the age of forty-seven, he had interests in several hotels – the British Hotel in Queen Street, the Imperial Hotel in Bourke Steet, and even a down-market miners' hotel in the goldfield town of Clunes.

The worthy Thomas Graham had been everything – from carpenter, shipwreck survivor, owner of punts on the Yarra, hotel-proprietor and consummate philanderer. After a brief interview, Cathy had her apprenticeship confirmed at eight pounds a year (slightly less than the going rate), courtesy of Thomas Graham. She was due to begin work in three days' time.

She lugged her box of survival treasures back to steerage deck for the further three days and two nights. She used those days, packing and unpacking her box of treasures, chatting excitedly to her orphan friends and bidding farewell to everyone, including Captain Boldrewood and the crew, and the rats, fleas and cockroaches. Three days later, with a sigh of relief and lugging her precious box, Cathy made her last trip down the gangway and loaded herself and her possessions aboard Thomas Graham's buggy. Then they clip-clopped their way from the docks towards Queen Street.

Cathy did her apprenticeship at the British Hotel, Queen Street. There is no evidence that Thomas Graham directed his amorous propensities towards our Cathy. As far as we know, she survived her seventeenth year with her virginity intact. In any case, Graham's gross porcine dimensions would have made him a totally unattractive proposition. In the egalitarian society of Australia, the girl had the undisputed right to say 'Yea' or 'Nay' to unwelcome attentions.

Cathy applied herself diligently to the needs of Graham's Queen Street hostelry establishment. With practised eye and nimble hands, she made beds, swept rooms, mopped floors, changed and washed linen, and occasionally opened her mouth to respond in her Irish brogue to the needs of guests. Life was pretty good. Entrepreneurs from the gold mine areas, including the rough, untutored, grime-encrusted men who had struck it lucky, were among the guests. Cathy became quite adept at fending off overnight propositions from sex-deprived miners. She was on the lookout for something more permanent than a one-night stand. Also, God was watching – twenty-four seven!

5

New Life in the Goldfields

Then it happened! It was August 1850. Seventeen-year-old Catherine's indentured term was coming to an end. Her boss, Thomas Graham, the consummate philanderer, had so far kept his distance. Maybe he thought that this skinny, not overly attractive Irish colleen did not meet his high expectations. Or maybe he was simply getting too long in the tooth for his erstwhile amorous pursuits. He had continued to expand in all directions. Cathy's Catholic hands-off morality continued intact.

One particular winter's day, she was busy mopping the corridor when she was accosted by an earnest-looking, not-so-young man with a sunburnt face. The typical, frustrated wannabe miner! One positive, she thought: he wasn't as begrimed as the others.

His technique was direct. He propositioned her, immediately and directly.

'How about it? Something permanent!' he said. 'Like marriage!' It caught her by surprise. Her heart fluttered. It was time for her lunch-break and some serious thinking. She didn't even know his name. Who cares about lunch? Who cares about serious thinking? She suddenly blurted out:

'OK! Why not? I'm sick of scrubbing floors.'

His response was, 'Right! Bewdy! It's a deal.' If only all marriage proposals were as simple!

Then he told her the whole story. He had come from the goldfields – a place called Clunes, where rumours festered about secret gold deposits on a property belonging to a gentleman by the name of Don Cameron. Apparently, a certain James Esmond (without the e), having recently returned from the Californian goldfields, fell in with landowner Don Cameron and staked the first official claim.

Meanwhile, following the rumours, our wannabe miner, also James by name, had been pottering around hoping to strike it lucky. There were prospective miners everywhere. Entranced by the rumours, James had joined the company of the hitherto unsuccessful prospectors. Some did strike it rich. Others did not – James included. Disillusionment followed him everywhere. Suddenly a brainwave! Maybe timber was the way to go. So James changed his aspirations from mining to timber-getting, responding to the special needs of the time. His full name was James Kirby.

James and Cathy's stories rang so many familiar bells. James hailed from Cork, a mere fifty-two miles from Dungarvan, though to travel fifty-two miles in the early 1800s was no mean feat. When James, who could read in a rudimentary way, showed illiterate Cathy their respective homes on a map of Ireland in the hotel dining-room, it was obvious to her that they were neighbours. As they chatted they discovered many common threads. There was their Irishness to start with, which included everything from accent to their shared Catholicity, and their common myths and legends. What Cathy saw was a husband-to-be who was an absolute 'Corker' in both senses of the word. So for all kinds of reasons, Cathy felt that her best option was to accept his proposal.

James' story was not dissimilar to Cathy's. His parents, John Kirby and Mary Burke, had lived and died in Cork. It was while they were still in their mid-forties, looking after a brood of ten children, that their number one son James made an unexpected decision. At the youthful age of roughly twenty, he decided to seek his fortune in a faraway land across the seas – Australia. As James subsequently learned, most of his family suffered the same fate as Cathy's family, dying of hunger and disease contracted during the devastating Potato Famine.

James was always rather ambivalent about his age. In those days, when illiteracy was so common, when the Irish were banned from attending school, and when the lucky ones survived on a hedge-row education, many of them never knew their exact date of birth. So they made it up. James claimed to have been born in 1821, making him eleven years older than Cathy. Cathy was not particularly concerned about age difference, as long as she got her man. As soon as her indentured time was up, she followed her man to the goldfields.

James and Cathy set up camp in the burgeoning tent city on the outskirts of Clunes. They started their timber-getting activities with an axe, a crosscut saw and one ox, usually known in Australia as a bullock. The main challenge was moving materials from one place to another. The bullock became their prime mover. A bullock was cheaper to buy and easier to manage than a draught horse. It could work for long hours and could cover up to fifteen miles a day. It made so much sense to invest in a bullock. So that's what they did.

For obvious reasons, they called their bullock 'Bullo'. They tethered him on a long rope attached to a tree not too far from their tent so that he could eat his fill during the night. They had commandeered a little patch of land a hundred yards away. When the grass became a patch of dry dust, Bullo's evening repast became an expensive bale of hay.

James and Cathy worked side by side felling ancient eucalypts, lopping branches, trimming, shaping, sorting out logs and choosing wide, flat, long strips of stringy bark suitable for roofs. The rest was firewood.

The lucky ones who struck gold set themselves up in central Clunes. The others hunkered down in their flimsy tents hoping for a change in fortune.

Four and a half months later, on 26 January 1851, sixty-three years to the day since Governor Phillip laid claim to Australia at Port Jackson, James and Cathy returned to Melbourne for the wedding. It was a simple affair at St Francis' Church, Lonsdale Street, in the heart of Melbourne town. It was in this same little church that St Mary MacKillop made her First Communion, and it was also here that Ned Kelly's parents were married a few months earlier. For us, Cathy's progeny, the icing on the cake was that here within the hallowed walls of St Francis' Church our James and Cathy were to be joined together in the sight of God in holy matrimony. How exciting it is to think that our ancestry was at this point thus legitimised!

James stood tall in a borrowed suit, looking like the proverbial fish out of water, accompanied by a dozen of his bewhiskered mining mates. Cathy had managed to rustle up a second-hand wedding dress, courtesy of her friend Shaelah. Supporting her was a respectable bunch of her ex-workhouse friends, including Beth and Shaelah, who were now married and bent on adding to Melbourne's ever-increasing population. Thomas Graham was also there, pompously declaring, 'I wouldn't have missed it for quids!' He sat in the front seat, regarding himself as a father figure to Cathy, dressed in his best suit with bowtie, top hat balanced on his knee. Being a 'Proddy' (a neologism, I believe), he wasn't able to join in 'Faith of Our Fathers' with the mainly Bog-Irish worshippers, but he insisted in doing a solo of 'The Holy City' at the end of the ceremony, inviting all to join in the chorus. As a gesture of inter-faith communion, they all did as they were bid and sang lustily: *'Jerusalem. Jerusalem, lift up your gates and sing.'* All were so happy for Cathy and James, who indeed lifted up their hearts and unreservedly gave them to each other.

They all pretended not to notice the bump beneath Cathy's wedding garb. But before the night was over, tongues began to wag.

One week later they were back at Tent City. It was then that the tell-tale symptoms became even more obvious. As well as the baby bulge and the missed periods, there was the morning sickness, swollen breasts, emotional outbursts and fatigue. It must have happened in the dark confines of the tent several months ago, maybe during their first week in Tent City, when they were in the early throes of passion often experienced by a male and female living in one tent.

The gold rush at Clunes was gathering momentum. Prospective miners, with hope in their eyes and their guts, were converging on Clunes. Industry of any kind required transport. James, the failed goldminer, was there to provide such transport.

James and Cathy now had a second bullock, which Cathy continued to call 'ox', plus a second-hand four-wheeled cart with squeaky wooden wheels. James had to explain to Cathy that two oxen aren't called two 'oxes'. Cathy was really pretty bright. She caught on quickly, reminding James not to patronise her. James buttoned his lip and got on with lugging logs. Cathy continued to be obstinately illiterate. But at least she agreed to call two oxes – two *bollocks*. James had to explain that these bullocks had been castrated and therefore bollocks was totally inappropriate. They were called *bullocks* not *bollocks*! Cathy got the message!

Cathy tried to work as hard as ever, but James put the brakes on.

'Take it easy, old girl. I want both you and the kid to survive this birth stuff!' Cathy's response was, in the words of a person I know so well:

'She's apples, old man. Relax.'

She could no longer work like a traction engine. Soon she had to give up the crosscut saw and log lifting. She had to content herself with managing the oxen, gathering twigs and doing the cooking. The good thing about life in the bush is that you don't have to worry too much about the niceties when engaging in domestic chores. A bowl of porridge for breakfast, bread and dripping and a chunk of meat left over from last night for lunch, and maybe Irish stew with a generous serving of spuds for dinner worked well in sating the pangs of familial hunger. Add to this an occasional swipe of the broom over the earthen floor and a once-a-week boiling of the copper pot for clothes washing kept Cathy more than busy enough.

The Clunes gold rush, heralded by James Esmond, had begun to gain momentum. James Kirby suddenly had more money in his pockets. Cathy now had a beautiful maternity dress decorated with flowers and butterflies – quite different from the workhouse garb, or indeed the dowdy hotel tunic. James had his eye out for two extra oxen to make a total of four and a second-hand jinker to replace the humble cart. To achieve this goal, he would have to work hard and save hard. Maybe cut back on the afternoon beer. And no more Irish whiskey!

The nine months passed quickly. One dark night, Cathy experienced a spasm of gut-wrenching abdominal pain.

'Owww! So this is what it feels like! Quick, Jimmy! What do I do now?' These were the days when the husband was supposed to know best.

'Call the mid-wife! Isn't that what yer supposed ter do? Maisie Thompson knows about this stuff.'

He immediately struck a match and lit the hurricane lantern. Maisie Thompson was two tents away. They woke her up from her slumber. Tripping over guy-ropes, she ran over to assist.

Cathy wailed on and off for two hours. James held her tightly, whispering such endearments as:

'Come on, colleen. You'll be right. It can't be as bad as all that!'

But it *was* as bad as all that. In fact it was worse! It was one of those back-the-front babies that got stuck half way. With an ear-piercing shriek, Cathy let Maisie Thompson know that she wanted this thing out, right now.

Baby's head was visible. A few wisps of reddish hair. It was a small baby. Maisie muttered two big words that sounded like 'placental deficiency!' She forced her long fingers in, grasped the baby's tiny head, and gently wriggled it out into the cold June air. She called James to bring a carving knife. James almost had a heart attack. His first response was:

'No! No! No!'

Maisie got impatient. 'Quick, James. Right now! Cut here!'

Maisie held the cord firmly with two hands and nodded to the space between. James did the deed. The baby started to squawk. Maisie smiled. James wept. Cathy laughed with relief.

They named her Mary-Anne. Cathy repeated endlessly, 'She's so beautiful!' But she wasn't really. There was something wrong. She was puny, a greyish colour, and wailed endlessly into the cold Clunes air. Over the next two weeks, her cries became more feeble. Then suddenly they stopped. Mary-Anne became still and cold.

The death of a newborn is utterly devastating. Cathy wailed long and with desperation. James buried this tiny wisp of humanity in a hole beside a gigantic gum tree. He wanted to print something special on a wooden plaque. He checked the spelling with his good mate John Hawkins before carving:

— WE LOVE YOU FOR ETERNITY, MARY ANNE —

But life trundles on. Big families were the dream as well as an inevitability for the average country-woman. Well-stocked families meant help on the farm, they were a consolation in your old age, and they worked as well as any superannuation scheme.

The gold kept rolling in as fossicking gold-diggers struck it rich. James benefitted on the sideline, raking in the occasional pound note – providing wood for fuel, humble shacks, cute log cabins, imposing edifices for the well-heeled, and supporting timbers for mine shafts. Initially, fossickers from the city scrabbled their way through the eucalypts, digging and scraping indiscriminately, looking for the stray, occasional nugget. On a sudden there was the odd gleam of gold just beneath the surface! 'Eureka!' they cried, in the words of Archimedes, the ancient Greek mathematician. They sweated, laughed, cheered, swore, wept and collapsed in sheer utter exhaustion at the end of each day. All good things come to an end. So says the mantra. Soon the elusive surface stuff ran out.

They then turned their attention to the creek – alluvial gold they called it. Using the easily purchased gold pan, they sluiced for the elusive gold deep within the gravel of the murky waters of the Clunes Creek. They rocked back and forth till the fleeting dream became reality – minute specks of gold, which they secreted in the pouch concealed beneath their shirts. Thousands of prospectors slaved optimistically, panning and sluicing till the creeks dried up and there was barely enough water left with which to moisten their dry lips. James had tried both methods, churning over sand and rocks endlessly, among the ancient trees and rapidly evaporating creek beds. No wonder he had decided that carting wood was a better option.

Meanwhile, frustrated prospectors turned to digging shafts, the remnants of which still exist amongst the hillocks of mine tailings at Clunes. The Port Phillip Mining Company finally moved in, typically excavating shafts to 200 feet, equivalent to a modest twenty-storey building. Not to be outdone, depths of 700 feet have been recorded in the area – more than the height of New York's Empire State Building. James' contribution to these mineshafts was marginal, including an occasional load of logs for securing mineshaft walls and as fuel for the stampers and boilers.

James now focused his attention on providing more satisfactory, permanent accommodation for Cathy and the family-to-be. He managed to scrape up enough capital to invest in a bush block in the forest, one hour inland from the present Clunes Cemetery. His block was in the foothills of Mount Beckworth, a few miles to the west of Clunes properly so called. He was two miles to the north as the crow flies from the cemetery, where he was ultimately to become a permanent resident.

James began clearing the trees and salvaging the timber on his five-acre bush block. He had spent all of his available funds on the block. 'How can I possibly afford to build a house? Milled timber costs a packet. And I'm stony broke!'

Then the brainwave. He had got the idea from a Canadian miner, a certain Gaspard Garnier, originally from Fraser Valley, British Columbia. They had met in the Bullock and Dray pub. When Gaspard heard James complaining about the high cost of milled timber, Gaspard told him about the Canadian way – the log cabin.

'It's easy as pie. You've got plenty of logs on your block. They're free for the taking – no buying milled timber … Cut 'em down, cut 'em up, notch the corners, stack 'em up, wedge 'em in place, bog the cracks with clay, slap on a bark roof, and Robert's yer aunty's husband!'

James thought, scratched his head, and thought a bit more. 'Yair', he said to himself, 'I've got more than enough stringybark, for sure. But they're bloody 'eavy, not like that pine they've got over in Canada. But I've got me two bullocks, me mates and plenty er six inch logs. And it's all fer nix. I'll give it a bash.' And he did!

He managed to scrounge a stash of the highly prized red ironbark for the posts and for horizontal logs touching the earth. Ironbark is known for its durability and resistance to rot. He supplemented this with logs of stringybark messmate, which grew prolifically on his block. It was accessible, cheap, strong, easy to cut, perfect for both walls and pitched roof. Its further advantage was it provided him with the long, wide slabs of bark that were ideal for covering the roof.

James knew all about timber. That was his profession. He was also quite adept at connecting pieces of timber in a useful and permanent way. He constantly reminded Cathy about how proud she must be to have such a wonderfully clever husband.

Cathy responded, 'Yeeee-s! But I would be even prouder if you bent your elbow a little less. You know what I'm talking about. It's one word that I *do* know how to spell – grog.'

Cathy loved her new house, and despite the little bit of teasing, she decided that her hubby James was not too bad either, notwithstanding his minor peccadillos. It was November 1852 when Cathy began to experience the familiar discomfort of morning sickness. In the words of the locals, 'she spewed her guts out', and laughed till she cried. James had been harnessing the four oxen for the day's work. Up till now, he could never understand how a woman could laugh and cry at the same time. Women are just weird! But he suddenly guessed how it was. So he followed suit. Now he understood what it was about women. 'Maybe we're not that different!'

The months flew by quickly. Everyone needed wood. His pockets were full of coins – a mix of pennies, shillings and sometimes florins. James couldn't keep up with the demand.

One night in July, the familiar scenario reoccurred. Abdominal pains. Close together. Big belly. Big baby. Heart in her mouth.

'Quick, James! He – or maybe she – is about to pop out. Come on belly, push! Maisie Thompson, where are you? I forgot. Back at Clunes.'

Too late. A deep breath. Push again! And out it popped. A male of the species. Snip. Scream. Wrap. Cuddle. Morphing from blue to red to Irish off-white.

'John Patrick Kirby – I baptise thee in the name of the Father and of the Son and of the Holy Ghost ...'

Father Patrick Geoghegan (later to become Bishop Geoghegan)

intoned the ritual words. Within the blink of an eye, John is a 'dinky-di' Aussie Catholic. He echoed his assent with an ear-piercing scream that reverberated from wall to wall within the confines of their adopted church, St Francis' in Melbourne city.

Why not in the Clunes church? The simple answer is that at that time there was no church in Clunes. History tells us that the first Catholic church in the Goldfields began as a tent in Bendigo in 1851. The following year, the miners built a makeshift bark and slab chapel – fifty-six miles from Clunes. 'Too far!' James and Cathy thought, and in any case not good enough for the Kirbys. They wanted their first-born to be baptised in style. So why not at St Francis', where they were married?

James and Catherine weren't regular churchgoers mainly because there was no church to go to. Given their Irish heritage, their Catholic religion helped identify them. They wanted nothing but the best for their offspring. For them the *best* was St Francis' in Melbourne, which they knew so well, for this was where they were married. So that's where John and their subsequent children were baptised.

History tells us that the Bendigo bark and slab chapel was replaced a few years later by a more up-market sandstone chapel, St Kilian's, the building of which was instigated by the forward-thinking German parish priest, Father George Backhaus. It was opened in 1858. The church of St Thomas Aquinas in Clunes did not eventuate until 1874. This was too late for the baptism of James' subsequent progeny. So James and Cathy continued to prefer to have their offspring baptised in style – at St Francis' Church, Melbourne.

James did not experience the kind of prosperity enjoyed by those fortunate gold-diggers who had struck it rich. But neither did he suffer the fate of the unlucky ones who scrabbled and scraped at clay and rock, day in day out, without ever experiencing the so-called luck of the Irish. James' log-carting business was steady as she goes. He insisted on cash in hand for work done. No credit. No empty promises. The challenge was to keep working steadily, resisting the temptation to join his bibulous mates for an afternoon tipple. Except maybe on Saturday night. Cathy reminded him, as gently as she dared, that they now had an extra mouth to feed.

Their basic log cabin needed a rustic table, a couple of stools and two real X-framed beds to replace the wooden crates and the pile of straw-filled palliasses in the corner. And luxury of luxuries, a cot for little Johnny!

The log cabin needed extending beyond the one basic all-purpose living space. In this reasonably large room, they prepared meals, dined, bathed in a small tub and bedded down each night. It was time for another large room specifically designated for sleeping. So James tacked on another log-cabin-styled appendage designed to accommodate the needs of his prospective traditional Irish family. They had demonstrated their capacity to procreate. Why not aim for a family of ten or twelve or whatever? The downside would mean more mouths to feed. But the upside is reflected in the oft-repeated adage about many hands making light work.

James' plan was to extend the house lengthways in the traditional way, to avoid the complication of pitching right-angled roofs with technically complicated valleys and gutters, which in any case don't work too easily for a bark slab roof. At the end of a day of hard timber-carting, with a glass of spirit-sustaining ale sitting on a nearby block of wood, James applied himself to the onerous task of adding a spacious bedroom to the basic log cabin. Time, work and his ample stash of timber enabled him to extend their living space in accordance with his forward-thinking master plan. Cathy, now a typical Aussie country wife, played her part lifting logs and filling in the gaps with a mix of mud and clay. She had become quite good at climbing ladders and quite adept at creating a reasonably watertight roof, consisting of superimposed layers of bark, courtesy of the surrounding stringybark trees.

Baby John had now graduated from breast milk to mashed potatoes and bread, washed down with beef broth, and a smidgeon of mutton whenever it was available. He lay on the stone floor, gooing and gaaing and smiling his gummy smile, which soon became a toothy grin. To Cathy's delight he was soon sitting, crawling and skidding along crab-like on his rear end. Then came the first few tentative steps, grasping at hands, legs and furniture. James applauded:

'That's ma boy!'

Cathy beamed and kootchy-kootchy-kooed. 'What a kid! And it's all our own work!'

Then the inevitable happened. What do you do when you snuggle into bed with your loved one, in an era when there was no radio, no TV, no electric light, no games of Scrabble and no reading yourself to sleep?

It is the cusp of autumn, 1854. Suddenly there were the familiar symptoms. Cathy would mysteriously burst into tears although she was overjoyed at the prospect of another 'bun in the oven'. Crazy stuff! Women! Then there was the potato thing. How could an Irish-woman suddenly hate potatoes? It had to be pumpkin or nothing! James would never understand women, despite his superior male experience and the advantage of an extra eleven or twelve years on this earth. He never really knew for sure, but he thought he was about thirty-three years of age, just like Jesus was when he died on the cross. Christians would therefore say that thirty-three was the prime of life. So James was all knowing, like Jesus. But he still would never understand women. Be that as it may, he would do his best.

'Cathy, my love, whatever you want, no matter how crazy, I'm there for you! But – no potatoes? Just pumpkin? How crazy can you get!'

But Cathy got her pumpkin. Lucky it was a good year for pump-kins. They grew prolifically outside the back door.

Access to lumber required travelling greater distances as they cut into accessible eucalypt forests. Gold mines, boilers and new houses had an insatiable hunger for eucalypt forests, which James and his fellow wood-carters knew as *the bush*, consisting primarily of gums of different species. They were called gums because they exuded copious quantities of gum or resin.

The bullocks continued to work slowly and steadily. Their limit was twelve to fifteen miles per day. James' simple knowledge of mathematics suggested that a four-bullock wagon was twice as efficient as a two-bullock wagon. So he loaded the wagon accordingly.

The wagon was much the same as a dray, although strictly speaking a dray didn't have sides. James used both names interchangeably.

James and Cathy soon slipped into the Aussie way of calling their timber conveyance 'the bullock wagon'. James became 'Jimmy, the Bullock Wagon Man'. It defined him; it was a way of life; it gave him a sense of power; and he loved his bullocks, his wagon and the steady income that came with them.

All of their mates constantly reminded James and Cathy that they were literally and metaphorically living on a gold mine. Although James rarely touched the yellow stuff, it was the source of his relative prosperity. Gold nuggets were hiding under the ground in hidden recesses waiting to be tapped by such as James. The key to life-long prosperity was about striking it rich. It was a combination of luck and hard work. But James had little confidence in luck. Nor was he too keen on hard work.

James was no fool. He was a numbers man. He concluded that mathematically the odds were against him. The prospect of sweating away endlessly, deep under ground, hour after hour, jarring every bone in your body in the forlorn hope of striking it rich didn't add up. He continued to resist the temptation to try his luck as a digger and decided to be happy with the safer option of carter, tapping into the needs of the miners. He saw his role essentially as that of a facilitator. So, applying this philosophy, James continued to embrace the relative comfort enjoyed by the essential-services, hard-working wood-carter.

James and Cathy never forgot their humble origins. They had risen from dirt-poor Irish stock. Sure, they had achieved an undreamt-of level of affluence, but it never went to their heads.

The flow-on principle applied. Individual miners, as well as large companies, needed support systems for their survival. James was part of that system. We read in the 1855 annual report of the Clunes Quartz Mining Company:

> *The Clunes quartz reefs have obtained a world celebrity for richness, quality of material and situation combining the advantages of an abundant supply of water <u>with contiguity of timber</u>.'*

The latter phrase refers very specifically to James and his contribution to the Clunes gold mining venture. By 1854, nuggets sitting under trees and gold dredged from rivers were a thing of the past. They were now accessing their gold by burrowing deep into the ground. Mine shafts needed timber supports: cave-ins spell disaster. It goes without saying: no timber, no mineshafts. Furthermore, there were the boilers and furnaces that drove the lifts, hydraulic machinery, stampers, smelters and blast furnaces that transformed gold dust and small shapeless clumps of the precious metal into manageable and quantifiable ingots. These processes and the accompanying machinery required heat, and the source of heat was wood and lots of it. And just as importantly, where there were people you needed houses, stables, fences, furniture, and horse- and bullock-drawn vehicles, of which timber was the main component. It was obvious that much depended on the work of the humble wood-carter.

Let's forget James, the woodcutter and carter, for the moment and take a look at the geology of the area. When we were at school, we learnt about the three types of rock – metamorphic, igneous and sedimentary. They were all to be found in the goldfields. Geological changes over the years tended to mix them up. In the Ballarat area, there was a predominance of slate, which took the form of layers of mud that were compressed till they became rock – more specifically, sedimentary rock. In the Clunes area it was mainly metamorphic – layers of rock, which by definition metamorphosed from rock that was primarily igneous to quartz. This geological metamorphosis was the result of heat, pressure and movement, which brought about both physical as well as chemical change. For some mysterious reason, metamorphic rock in the area turned out to be auriferous – layers of compressed rock having veins of gold in between – everything from gold dust to the occasional small ingot.

Once the surface nuggets had been accessed, attention was turned to creeks and rivers, where miners worked with pans, sluice boxes and cradles. Surface miners worked primarily in Creswick Creek, an offshoot from Tullaroop Creek to the north that ran through Clunes before disappearing into the ground four miles south at Glendonnell. The hot sun, the absorbent soils and the needs of human beings took their toll on inland creeks. Initially, at Clunes itself, there was enough water to activate the sluices. This rather amateurish process of gold accessing soon ran out of the huge quantities of water needed for sluicing. On the north edge of Clunes, they turned to digging shafts hundreds of feet in depth, adding side tunnels whenever they discovered an auriferous vein. Even then, when the rains came, the miners were faced with the challenging task of pumping water from the deep shafts that had been created by enterprises large and small, but primarily by the Port Phillip Mining Company. Striking the balance between an excess of underground water and water needed on the surface was not always easy.

James supplied timber on a needs basis. The strongest and more reliable timber of a specified length and dimension went to the big companies for such life and death situations as vertical and horizontal props used in deep mines. Next came the timber millers who processed timber of certain species and dimensions suitable for milling and housing construction. Then came hardwood odds and sods cut to six-foot lengths and suitable for boiler consumption. Whatever was left over was used for domestic purposes: fuel for fireplaces and wood stoves. James was never short of customers.

Corrugated iron was in. Bark roofs were out. Bark roofs leaked and required too much maintenance. They were laid in multiple layers but they still leaked. They split open under the fierce rays of the sun, they rotted when wet, and they attracted insect infestation. On the upside, they were cheap and easily accessed. But installing them required a lot of time and 'mucking about', as James wisely observed. You had to place a network of logs over the layers of bark to hold them in place. So James became fixated on the new corrugated iron. The special advantages of this material were that it was light, strong and affordable. It was the corrugations that gave this new roofing material its strength, lightness and rigidity. Galvanised iron had been the go since the early 1840s. Originally, rust was the problem for unprotected steel roofs, but hot-dip galvanising had been invented in England in the 1820s by English engineer, Henry Robinson Palmer. Hence rust was no longer a problem, given galvanised iron's thirty year plus lifespan. In fact, it became the favoured roofing material in country Australia by the early 1840s. So James replaced his economical but inefficient bark roof with a corrugated galvanised wrought iron roof. The light-weight, cheaper version – mild steel galvanised roof sheeting – had not yet been invented.

At the height of summer, 22 December 1884, the familiar pains occurred. Cathy thought that she was now an expert at this childbirth business. This was to be her third. She remembered the trauma of the first child, Mary Anne, who didn't survive the first two weeks. John, her second child, was now eighteen months, a beautifully energetic toddler, tip-ping over cups, crying vociferously over spilt milk, tripping over James' boots, grabbing the two pairs of adult legs that dominated his world.

This time, Cathy was well prepared. Midwife Maisie Thompson belonged to the past. Maisie lived on the outskirts of Clunes, miles away from Mount Beckworth. But matronly Agatha Trumble, although she was C of E and therefore not of the Holy Roman Church, had a good reputation for bringing babies into the world. The special advantage was that Agatha was a neighbour and a good one at that. She and Cathy often chatted over the fence about babies and motherhood. Aggie had a multitude of stories about birthing tricks and positions. She favoured the age-old, traditional 'on-your-back, legs-apart pozzy', where the midwife can see what's going on. While gravity apparently supported the new-fangled ideas about gravity-assisted standing, kneeling and squatting positions, she convinced Cathy that the supposedly more comfortable, lying-down position was the best for everyone, despite the advice of the birthing pundits. So that's how new babe Catherine came into this world. It was a long and painful process because baby Catherine was a big seven pounder, not that they had scales out there on Mount Beckworth. But Matron knew from experience. On the evening of 23 December, not-so-little Catherine squeezed her way into this world. She was a bonny, brown-haired babe who screamed her lungs out as James, the self-appointed expert, cut the cord.

The score was now one boy and one girl. Cathy had an eye to the future.

'Jimmy, my dear, it's time to look ahead. I know yer want a big traditional Irish family. And I know yer love our time in bed together. Let's face it: we do more than sleep!'

'Wha'd'yer mean, Cath old girl?' he replied teasingly.

'None of this old-girl stuff. I know you won't tell me your real age. But judging by the wrinkles, you are at least ten years older than me. And ...'

'OK. Maybe. So whadr'yer gettin' at, my not-so-old girl?'

'Well, I reckon I'm about twenty-one. So far, it's been one kid a year. I could have another twenty-five of 'em – particularly with me having a randy husband like you.'

'Get ter the point, Cath, old … I mean, young girl.'

'I mean you better get stuck into that extra room! Otherwise, no more hanky-panky! We're gonna need a boys' room as well as the girls' one. So get cracking!'

Jimmy loved playing the innocent with his darling wife, if for no other reason than to engage in a highly entertaining, point-scoring exercise. And the bonus was twofold – first, more quality time in bed with his beloved, and, second, negotiating more hours with his mates at the pub. The Bullock and Dray Tavern was the favourite haunt for James and his mates. But he had to compromise. Drinking and building don't work too well together. He'd need to rationalise as well as compromise.

'OK, Cathy, me darl. I'll get me mates from the pub ter help me lift a few of them big bastards. We'll stick with the log cabin idea – logs, logs and more logs – the real good'uns that'll last us out. Ironbark for posts and sleepers. Just like last time!'

'Righto, Jimmy! You sure know yer timbers. I 'ave every confidence in you. You'd better get cracking!' A little bit of priming up works a treat!

'OK Cath. I'll get the boys over and we should start sometime this week.'

Cathy replied, 'Sounds good to me! But, remember my rule about no grog on the job. No gettin' sozzled! Work and grog don't go together!'

James assumed his special sad, 'poor me' persona. 'If we can't have an occasional beer to lubricate our stiff joints as well as our tonsils, we can't get the job done.'

'All right! A compromise. You can each 'ave a couple of sips from the keg stashed in our bedroom at the end of the day, but only if yer've done a good day's work! And I'll be the judge!' James nodded a noncommittal assent. It's called a negotiated compromise.

So it happened. James and his mates extended the house another fifteen feet. For the base and posts they used their well-practised methodology – hard-to-get ironbark logs, and for above the base they used more common stringybark, brought in by his four oxen. They would now have a good-sized third room for the girls. The second room was for John and the odds and sods and any other prospective brothers. The first room was still James and Cathy's room as well as the nursery.

James was on a building spree.

'Cath, me luv, we've got a few extra pounds in the kitty. We've still got the rest of that keg in our bedroom to help lubricate our tonsils and our joints. I've still got my real good mates out there ready to give a hand. We'll do it proper while we're on a roll.'

So over the next few weeks, James and his mates finished the girls' bedroom, and added a long sloping veranda at the front, and a purpose-built washhouse and workshop at the back, with low lean-to roofs on both sides. It was now a typical Aussie farmhouse. James declared portentously:

'When yer on a roll, hang in there and get it done. That's the Irish way!' Maybe or maybe not! Most Poms wouldn't agree. Maybe James was the exception.

The other aspect of doing it the Irish way was celebrating in style with a half a keg of beer when the job was done. For once Cathy was lost for words. They offered her a glass of the good stuff. She tasted it, screwed up her face, handed it back to James.

'Yuuuuuk!'

Not wishing to waste it, James downed the rest in one gulp!

Over the next ten years, James and Catherine managed to generate another four children, making a total of seven, if you count Mary Anne who died shortly after birth. John was number two. But for some mysterious reason that still has geneticists scratching their heads, the next five were female. Is it the luck of the draw, or is there some other mysterious pattern that continues to elude the pundits? All those modern stories about when and how, diet, position and boxer shorts don't seem to make any difference to the basic 50/50 statistic. Maybe it's God making decisions in his own incomprehensible God-like way to help balance the books. For James and Catherine, five girls in succession would have been a little like winning modern-day Tatts Lotto in reverse.

In those days, it was assumed that boys' prospective work output was superior to that of the average girl, and therefore the birth of a boy was an occasion for special rejoicing. Most modern males wouldn't dare expound such a proposition. Be that as it may, despite his initial disappointment, James shrugged his shoulders and declared that his daughters' value as well as their work output would match that of any male – any day. Cathy couldn't agree more. To emphasise her point, she not too subtly declared that the girls she knew did not waste their time swilling beer with their mates. Whoops! It was on for young and old – an age-old idiom that was particularly appropriate given their eleven years' difference in age.

James was of the school of thought that wisdom grew with age. It was time for him to dig in his heels. How dare Cathy challenge his inalienable right to tipple with his mates! With as much conviction as he could muster, he made the point that a male's superior work output put him way ahead. It was both logical and fair that they needed a little extra lubrication. An occasional beer or two or three was both an incentive and a reward. Cathy won the day by matching her fourteen hours a day against his paltry eight.

He conceded: 'OK, Cath, old … I mean, young girl! I give in. Maybe we're even stevens! Fair enough! I'll half it – down to maybe four beers a day, except on Sundays. Just maybe!'

It is often suggested that excessive alcohol intake can reduce potency. It did not work that way for James. And coupled with Cathy's corresponding libido, the inevitable came to pass. On 23 December 1857, Catherine Junior exuberantly burst her way into this world. She was to be known as Catherine, to distinguish her from Cathy, the mum. She was so like her mother with her get-up-and-go energy. She was full of new tricks. At two months, she would stretch out on her back, smile expansively and gummily, clutch at the air, do her one kick routine or her special two-at-a-time trick, skidding forward on her back on the threadbare mat, giggling as she went.

'That's ma girl!' crowed James. Cathy just smiled contentedly with a tear in her eye.

Undoubtedly because of the procreative energy of the Irish, the kids kept coming. After baby Catherine, for whom mum Cathy had such high hopes, who should grace the scene in May 1857 but little Margaret, Cathy's fourth child to survive the throes of childbirth. She would have weighed in at six pounds two ounces if they had had scales in those days. Margaret was a gentle, sad-eyed little babe. She sucked away blissfully at her mother's milk for the next twelve months. No tantrums, no extreme emotions, certainly no trouble, and not too many smiles. When daddy or mummy tickled her tummy, there were no gales of laughter as with the other two. Most of the time, she lay quietly staring at the tin roof. No teething tantrums. Just the occasional, non-committal, enigmatic Mona Lisa smile. She didn't learn to walk till she was eighteen months. She was the classic late developer. She bided her time, and when she finally reached toddler status, there were no angry episodes as with the others. Apart from the occasional spilt milk, tripping face down on the uneven floorboards, the classic blood nose and the split lip, she took it all in her stride and continued to be the *good* little girl!

Number five vociferously announced her presence two and a bit years later, in June 1859. They named her Elizabeth. In no time little Lizzy's special personality began to emerge. She was quite different from delicate little Margaret. She was bouncy and exuberant, and she laughed like a hyena and squawked with enthusiasm and *joie de vivre* whenever her siblings gave her the roughhouse treatment. James would throw her up into the air towards the rafters, catching her in time before she hit *terra firma*. Lizzy's response every time was to laugh uproariously. She loved her food as much as she loved mother's milk. She had big strong teeth and she bit hard and with conviction, prompting Cathy to wean her at ten months. At eighteen months, Lizzy was often seen 'helping' around the house. So Cathy nicknamed her 'my little helper'. From the age of two, Liz loved nothing better than helping Mum with the broom, spreading the dirt rather than sweeping it, and all too often poking her siblings in the eye. But they all loved Little Liz. John, now seven years old, wallowed in his role of the protective big brother.

James and Cathy had not yet finished with their procreating games. It was time for another boy, said James, but God saw differently. Less than two years after the arrival of Lizzie, number six was on the way. It was early autumn, 28 March 1861, when Annie first saw the light of day. A few wisps of black hair and out she slithered, quite effortlessly. Cathy was getting so good at churning out new-borns. Annie opened her large brown eyes and blinked twice, dazzled by the light of the outside world. Annie was the dark-haired beauty, sparkling eyes, regular features and a cute little button nose. Everyone adored her and spoiled her rotten. From the start she was cuddled and cossetted – the perfect way to turn out a spoilt brat. But it was not to be. Annie had a gentle, accommodating, if somewhat serious, nature.

6

Court Appearance

It happened towards the end of 1861 – a minor blip in their otherwise blissful life. Annie, their latest acquisition, was now a delightful eight months old and smiling benignly at the world around her. It had been a good day – just short of two tons of stringybark, cut to boiler-friendly lengths, destined for the hungry mining stampers at Clunes.

'Yep! Johnny m' boy, we done a pretty good day's work.'

Johnny's response echoed his dad's: 'Yep Da, we done a real good day's work!'

They unhitched the team of four bullocks and temporarily tethered them to a stand of trees at the back of the pub, as was James' wont.

'Off you go, Johnny! Here's a penny for yer piggy bank! As I said before, yer done real good for an eight-year-old! Tell mum I'll be 'ome late.'

It had been a thirsty summer's day. James was exhausted and his all-consuming thirst, as usual, needed to be slaked. It was now mid-afternoon when James, well clear of Cathy's watchful eye, joined his mates at the Bullock and Dray pub. It was time to reward himself for the two tons of lumber. He couldn't wait to slake his thirst with a pint or two of the life-sustaining amber fluid.

Three hours later, James staggered out of the pub and re-hitched the bullocks to the dray. The bullocks under the guidance of Bullo, the boss bullock, set off for home. James had a mini-nap over the intervening two miles between the pub and home. He was awakened suddenly by the familiar voice of his dear one.

Cathy had heard the crunch of wheels on the gravel. James staggered towards the house smiling benignly. Cathy, not to be placated, emerged from the house and shrilly gave him the rounds of the table.

'I don't want a boozy slob for a husband! Here I am home alone slaving over a hot stove with five grumpy kids under my feet, whinging repeatedly, "Where's Dad?", while you're out there boozing with yer mates.'

James tried in vain to placate her.

'Fair go, Cath! I just wanted to celebrate today's great stash of lumber, two tons of it, with a few of me mates. Money in our pockets, food on the table, and a new dress for mi darlin' wife! What's wrong with that?'

Cathy kept on. 'I've had a gut-full. You know what yer can do with yer dress! In any case I hate yellow! It's always bloody yellow! I'm sick of yer Irish blarney.'

James hadn't finished, 'Come on, Cathy, me darl. It's all about you and the kids – especially you, me lovely Cathy.'

Cathy had had enough. She would really teach him a lesson this time.

'Don't try to butter me up, yer drunken slob! Get out of my house. Right now! No dinner for you tonight, Jimbo! And yer can sleep in the back yard with yer precious bullocks. It's time yer learnt a lesson!' It was 'Jimbo' whenever she was in a stink.

James staggered drunkenly into the yard, unhitched the four bullocks, tethered them in a slapdash huff to a nearby tree. There were a few blades of grass beside the track, which he supplemented with half a bale of hay. Then he collapsed on the ground under the tree beside his bullocks and promptly fell into a deep sleep, snoring stertorously.

A half-bale of hay wasn't enough. Bullo the bullock and his three bovine companions were known for their insatiable appetite. Bullo was the largest of the team and habitually called the shots. The four of them were tethered together and attached to one tree. It so happened that Bullo and his three friends rather cleverly 'untethered the tether and made off for town still tethered together' (as James later explained to his mates), in search of a more ample repast. They followed the well-worn track towards the stamping mill where they were accustomed to a good feed while James unloaded the wood for the boilers. Unfortunately, they took the customary path through the middle of town, where they were waylaid by Constable Macnab, a take-no-prisoners Scotsman. Macnab, true to his name, summarily arrested the said stray bullocks.

The following day, James now sober and in a panic, started to make enquiries of his neighbours. George Atwell smugly declared:

'Yer know, it's funny yer should mention it! I saw four stray bullocks, still harnessed together, headin' for town!'

James was annoyed. 'Well, why didn't yer stop 'em?'

George responded, 'I knew they couldn't be yours, given how fussy yer are at tethering yer bullocks.'

'Bollocks! Ye'r a real bastard when yer wanna be!' responded James in a fit of anger.

James jogged two miles to town and reluctantly decided to consult the local constabulary. His good mate George accompanied him to offer moral support. At the same time, George didn't want to miss out on a good story to share with their mates at the pub. Constable Macnab immediately put two and two together. 'Not you again, James Kirby. It's time you learnt a lesson! Your bullocks stay in the clink for the moment. You'll also pay for the bale of hay they gorged themselves on last night. See you in court, two o'clock this afternoon.' James fumed, swore vociferously like a true bullocky, and twiddled his thumbs till 2.00 pm.

We are now in the Clunes Police Court. It was 23 December 1861.

Both magistrates, J. D. Moore and P. Mark, Esquires, were on duty, dealing with cases of public drunkenness, petty theft, abusive language in public, a dog chasing horses, and the list goes on. Two o'clock came and went. Finally, at 3.30, James was summoned. James' case was easy. No questions asked. Summary slamming of gavel! Magistrate J. D. Moore just wanted to go home to the wife and kids.

'That will be a total of three shillings and sixpence! Next, please!'

James mumbled, 'I haven't got that on me right now.'

The judge coughed impatiently. 'Don't waste my time, Kirby! If you don't cough up quickly, we'll round it up to five shillings. Failing that it's the clink!'

Lucky for James, his mate George reached into his voluminous pockets and found the required three shillings and sixpence amongst a mix of one pound notes and florins.

'Thanks George, old mate! I owe you big time!'

The story of James' runaway bullock was recorded in the *Creswick and Clunes Advertiser*, 24 December 1861, where there was a three-line summary of the said bullocks running amok in the town of Clunes. His misdemeanour and the subsequent penalty were there in print for his friends and clients to see – not that James minded too much. It made a good story to share with his mates at the Bullock and Dray.

TOWN INSPECTOR v JAMES KIRBY
Allowing four bullocks to wander
in the streets on the 14th instant;
fined 1s and 2s 6d costs.

The Babes Keep Coming

It was time for another roll of the dice. James' oft repeated mantra was, 'Plenty more where that one came from!' Cathy meanwhile struggled to keep up with four little kids under seven. No washing machine, drier, vacuum cleaner, gas stove or electric iron in those days!

Most of her housekeeping activities depended on a wood fire, a bucket of water, with an occasional dash of lye soap. At least Catherine and Margaret were old enough to help with the fetching, carrying, washing, sweeping and setting the table. John was little help with household chores as he was off every day helping James in the wood-carting business. He was good at holding the reins, gathering sticks, and yelling out in his decisive soprano voice, 'Giddyup!' and 'Whoa there!' at the appropriate time. So at least Cathy didn't have to worry about looking after John. He was his da's responsibility.

Meanwhile in the marital bed, at the end of each day, Cathy and James continued to give their full attention to what they did and loved best – procreating. Surely it was time for another boy. John would dearly love a brother to climb trees with, and James, who was heading for something like forty, desperately wanted at least two sons to inherit the thriving wood-carting business. But it was not to be. The first of July 1863 heralded the birth of yet another daughter, making it five in a row.

Ellen was number seven. Ellen was six days overdue. Aggie Trumble, the midwife, had been in and out as they awaited the advent of Cathy's seventh. As usual, it all happened without a hitch. After six successful births, Cathy had become quite good at churning out babies. This was the fifth girl in a row! James stifled his disappointment.

'It looks like it's still me and James on the wagon, I mean dray.' A slip of the tongue! *Being on the wagon* was an expression that James tried not to use, especially when Cathy was around. After all, as a good dad, he would have to celebrate Ellen's arrival with a drink or three with the mates.

After the ritual snip, there came the predictable metamorphosis from blue to red to white. Ellen, like the others, greeted the world on that cold, wintry night with an ear-piercing, heart-rending scream, following the age-old human custom of telling the world of her arrival. Unlike us humans, animals tend to make their appearance quietly and unobtrusively. Maybe being number seven, with its special biblical significance, added to the drama. As it turned out, Ellen, at number seven, was to be the last of James' offspring. And what a beautiful babe she was! Just like Annie, except for the colour of her hair. Her wisps of auburn locks, startled blue eyes and rosy lips heralded the arrival of another prospective candidate for the annual Clunes Baby Beauty Contest.

James continued to cut, cart and deliver wood, adding to his fund of pounds, shillings and pence. As the house had expanded, so did Cathy's stock of kitchenware and assorted knick-knacks – a box of second-hand cutlery, a stack of plates, dishes and cups, most of them chipped and of assorted shapes and colours. She purchased her kitchen utensils from the Clunes market, which the sellers repeatedly assured her were 'cheap at twice the price'. Cathy believed them. Her pride and joy was a cast-iron frypan, not to mention an enormous two-handled saucepan, and, to top it off, a generously proportioned earthenware flower-pot. There were also extra cots and beds for the growing family, all of them second-hand, to which she added a chunky bushman's table and eight non-matching chairs for the family of eight, counting the baby, plus a few extra for visitors.

The Kirby family home was all too often besieged by the inevitable bevy of neighbouring housewives – a mix of the hassled, the shy and the garrulous, who popped in for a cuppa. Added to Cathy's friends, there were James' fellow wagoners and drinking partners, who knew they were always welcome to share an ale or two, despite being under Cathy's watchful eye to ensure it was indeed nothing more than an ale or two.

Most importantly, James' team of bullocks had grown from four to six to eight making a considerable hole in James' pocket. But it was worth it as he had now doubled the amount of timber he could carry in one trip. Depending on the condition and gradient of the road, they could handle a load of a good three tons of bush timber. Their normal pace on flat ground was about three miles an hour. At a pinch, they could manage fifteen miles a day. Given that there was still a good supply of timber around the Mount Beckworth area where James lived, he didn't have to go too far for timber. James' bullock team was more versatile than some of the fourteen to eighteen bullock teams seen on long straight roads. He was able to negotiate tighter bends with his middle-sized team of eight, which were particularly suited to Mount Beckworth's winding roads.

Money was still tight even though James now more or less owned his own house, his dray and his bullocks. He survived on Irish blarney, promises and sundry loans from gullible and generous mates. Now and again, profiting from good deals with the gold mines, given their insatiable appetite for fuel for their furnaces, as well as from felling and disposing of trees for a couple of well-heeled customers, he managed to pay his bills. Nevertheless, he was lucky if he earned two pounds a week. By the time he had paid household bills, including food and clothing for his family of eight, there wasn't much left for his ritual daily couple of pints of the Phoenix Brewery's finest. James and Cathy were in survival mode most of the time until that day of total disaster early in the year of 1864.

Dungarvan Workhouse – where Catherine and her parents, Andrew and Mary, were assigned during the Potato Famine. Both her parents died there.

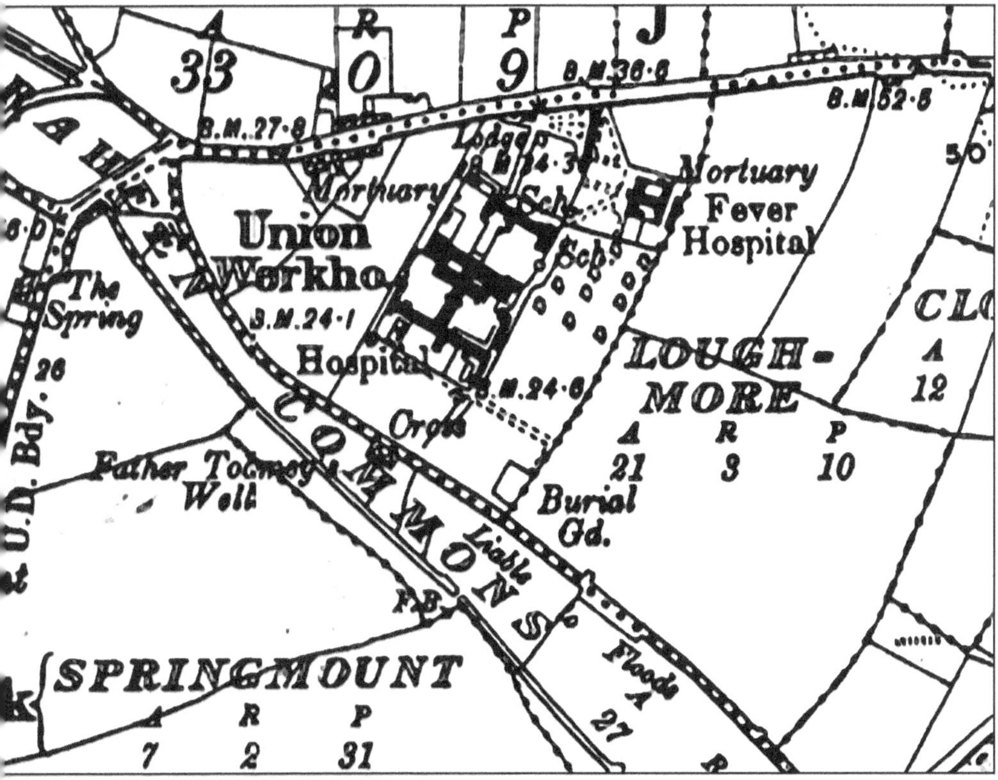

Map showing the Union Workhouse of Dungarvan, where Catherine was incarcerated, and the Fever Hospital, where both parents died.

Princes Pier, Melbourne, where the inmates of the Orphan Ship New Liverpool disembarked, 9 September 1849.

The portly Thomas Graham, licensee of the British Hotel, Queens Street Melbourne, where Catherine was indentured for twelve months before meeting James Kirby.

Francis' Church, Lonsdale Street, Melbourne, Victoria's first Catholic church and the place ...thy and James were married.

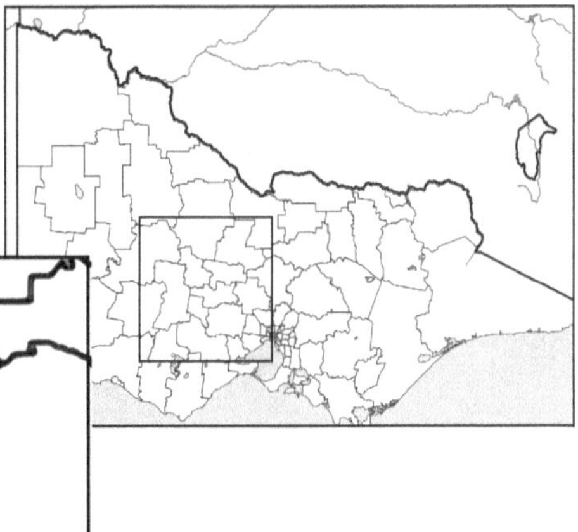

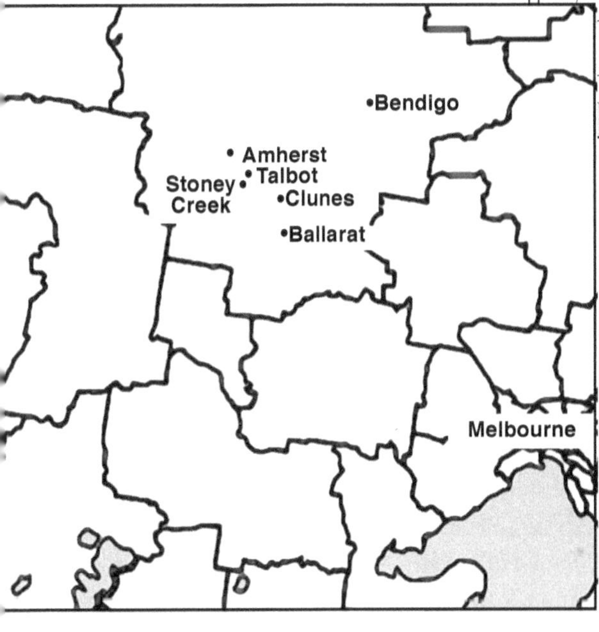

Bendigo

Amherst

Talbot

Stoney Creek

Clunes

Ballarat

Melbourne

Map of the Central Victoria goldfields (towns in approximate locations).

Tent cities such as this one sprung up on the Victorian goldfields. It was in one at Clunes that Catherine and James spent their first eighteen months before building their log and thatch cabin.

James and his bullock team setting off for a day's work.

1879. Marriages solemnized in the District of *Talbot*

No. in Register	When and where married.	Name and Surname of the Parties.	Condition of the Parties.			Birthplace.
			Bachelor or Spinster. If a Widower or Widow, State at Decease of former Wife or Husband.	Children by each former Marriage.		
				Living.	Dead.	
510	On the sixteenth day of December 1879 Talbot	James Edwin Barrett / Annie Kirby	Bachelor / Spinster			Alma, Maryborough, Victoria / Clunes Victoria

I, *John McNicol*, being *Presbyterian Minister*

do hereby certify, that I have this day, at *Talbot* duly celebrated Marriage between *James Edwin Barrett, miner, Talbot* and *Annie Kirby, Domestic Servant, Talbot* after Notice and Declaration duly made and published, as by law required (and with the written consent of *of the Brides mother Catherine Kirby*).

Dated this *sixteenth* day of *December* 1879.

Signature of Minister, Registrar-General, or other Officer *John McNicol*

Marriage certificate for J.E. and Annie.

SCHEDULE B.

DEATHS in the District of *Clunes* in the Colony

4

When and where Died.	Name and Surname, Rank or Profession.	Sex and Age.	(1) Cause of Death, (2) Duration of last Illness, (3) Medical Attendant by whom certified, and (4) when he last saw Deceased.	Name and Surname of Father and Mother, if known, with Rank or Profession.
Fifth January 1864 Talbot Road near Clunes	James Kirby — Wood Carter	Male 41 Years.	Internal Injuries caused by bullock dray passing over the body. Certified by Coroner —	Father's name not known. Mary Kirby formerly Burke
Twenty-fifth February	Sarah Ann —	Female 8 Years.	Shock to the nervous system caused by deceased being accidentally burnt by fire on her —	Alexander Kempfer Miner

Death certificate of James Kirby, who died in 1864, run over by his own bullock cart. James was buried in an unmarked grave in Clunes Cemetery.

SCHEDULE D.

1883

MARRIAGES solemnized in the District of *Clunes*
in the Colony of Victoria.

No. in Register.	Where and when Married.	Name and Surname of the Parties.	Condition of the Parties.			Birthplace.
			Bachelor or Spinster. If a Widower or Widow, Date of Decease of former Wife or Husband.	Children by each former Marriage.		
				Living.	Dead.	
7	June 1st 1883 Clunes Hospital	George Lawson Catherine Kirby	Widower Mt Rowan — Widow 1863	6 3	— 2	Buckinghamshire England Walford Ireland

I, *William Betten*, being *Bible Christian Minister* do hereby certify that I have, this day, at *the Clunes Hospital* duly celebrated Marriage between *George Lawson Farmer of Stony Creek* and *Catherine Kirby* after Notice and Declaration duly made and published, as by law required (and with the written consent of ______________________).

Dated this *first* day of *June* 188*3*

Signature of Minister, Registrar-General, or other Officer *William Betten*

Rank or Profession.	Ages.	Residence.		Parents.	
		Present.	Usual.	Names. (Mother's Maiden Name.)	Father's Rank or Profession.
Farmer	57	Stony Creek but now Resident of the Clunes Hospital	Stony Creek	William Lawson. Deborah Lawson Maiden Name (Lawson)	Farmer
Domestic	44	Stony Creek	Stony Creek	Andrew Coughlen Mary Coughlen Maiden Name (Kelly)	Farmer

Marriage, *by Licence*, was solemnized between us { *George X Lawson* } *Catherine X Kirby* according to the *rules of the Bible Christian Church*

Witnesses { *William Clunes* } *Elizabeth Kirby*

Marriage certificate of Catherine and George Lawson.

Death by Bullock Dray

It was the height of summer – Saturday 5 January 1864. Since it promised to be a hot day, James was up with the birds. Cathy prepared his breakfast of porridge, a slice of toast smothered in homemade plum jam, washed down with a ti-tree infusion that he had recently learnt about from the local Aborigines. James was on the road by 7.30 am with ten-year-old John. He picked up his mate James Ryan on the way. They drove one and a quarter miles from the foot of Mount Beckworth where they lived towards the main Ballarat-Maryborough Road. At the junction marked by the Bullock and Dray pub, they turned left and continued for another one and a quarter miles. At the logging site they proceeded to load the timber as pre-arranged with the timber-cutters. The January sun blazed down upon them mercilessly, but they worked tirelessly and had the dray loaded to capacity just after midday. They were back at the Bullock and Dray one hour later. James did not unhitch the bullocks from the dray. He tethered them on a grassy patch to the left of the Telegraph Road, a side service road to the left of the main Mount Beckworth Road, leaving them with such instructions as 'Whoa!' and 'Stay!'

James' pockets were empty. He intended to deliver this load of timber after a quick drink with his fellow-carter mates, the three Johns – John Raynes, John Hawkins and John Jones – at the Bullock and Dray. He depended on the generosity of Raynesy, Hawko and Jonesy to shout him a drink or two or three.

John knew from experience that two drinks became three or four or maybe eight, and that a half-hour became four. So ten-year-old Johnny headed for home. Despite his loyalty to his dad, sitting round for hours in the sun was not an option. Home he dawdled, reaching Cathy and family by 3.00 pm.

In the course of four hours, James managed to down his ritual eight beers. Meanwhile the oxen, weary of the flies and the heat, slipped the tether and headed for home.

The Bullock and Dray clock struck six.

'OK, boys …' declared the publican. 'That's it! See yer tomorrow!' It was six o'clock closing in those days. They downed their last beer and headed for the door.

'OK, Raynesy,' declared James. 'Let's go to your place – fer one fer the road!'

John Raynes' place was next to the pub. There they topped up with another two. By 6.30 pm James was staring regretfully at the bottom of an empty beer glass.

'Cathy will be spitting chips!' Without too much conviction he churned out his customary mantra: 'Home James and don't spare the horses!' The distinction between bovine and equine was not that important. They performed the same function. So off they went, heading for home.

Much to his horror, when he reached the familiar shady patch beside the Telegraph Road, it was obvious that the oxen and his load of timber were no longer there. Despite his slightly inebriated state, he put two and two together, and set off at a run up the telegraph track.

Ten minutes later, puffing and panting and slightly the worse for wear from his afternoon of tippling, he caught up with the bullocks and dray. James shouted out the ritual 'Whoa there!' But the oxen with their heads set for home kept moving, either because they didn't hear James' slurred commands over the rumble of the wheels, or because they were so fixated on getting home for food and water that they were prepared to risk James' wrath. Fortunately for them, the stockwhip was stashed high on the dray.

Then disaster struck ever so quickly. James made the fatal mistake of running in front of the left front wheel in his attempt to mount the dray. Normally he would never take such a risk. His alcohol intake affected his judgement. It is part of our DNA for us males to tempt fate. It was a risk that led to disaster. James slipped or tripped on the stony road and fell under the front wheel. A steel wagon wheel and three tons of timber are particularly unforgiving.

Each wheel had been carefully crafted by Wal Berrison the wheelwright, with strong wooden spokes supporting a sharp-edged steel rim guaranteed to cut through any living creature that fell in its path. James was nearly chopped in half by the merciless cutting action of that left front wagon-wheel. The bullocks continued blissfully on their way, unaware of the lifeless body of their erstwhile boss.

When the bullocks and the driverless wagon arrived home, Cathy assumed that James had sent them ahead on their own. These bullocks were well trained and certainly knew their way home. Cathy guessed that he had decided to stay at a mate's place for the night. This was the most obvious explanation amongst several other possible scenarios. She would give him the rounds of the table when he finally made it home the following day!

But the reality was that he didn't stagger, totter or even walk home that night. Deep down Cathy had a weird presentiment gnawing at her insides.

At six o'clock the following morning, Sunday, Cathy sent young Johnny to follow the Telegraph Road back towards the Bullock and Dray. He saw it when he was halfway between home and the pub. To his absolute horror, ten-year-old John was confronted with the traumatic sight of a motionless, familiar figure stretched out on his back, knees bent, arm twisted on an impossible angle, with bloody face and eyes still open staring at him sightlessly. John wailed as any grief-stricken ten-year-old would do and ran sobbing home to share the gruesome scenario with his mother.

Cathy, distraught and guilt-ridden given her negative thoughts and recent tirades, ran the three-quarters of a mile in record time along the Telegraph Road led by her son. John directed her to James' inert body. She knelt on the ground and hugged her husband unashamedly. Sobbing uncontrollably she kept repeating:

'James, my darling James! I hate you, God! What have you done to my darling James?' Quite different from last night's tirade!

It did not take long for friends, authorities and stickybeaks to gather round. James' three drinking partners were first on the scene, each with his own version of the drinking spree and subsequent events. Naturally they sought to give a positive account of their own bar-room habits as well as whatever mitigating circumstances related to their partner, James. They did not lie, as they were under oath, but they were prepared to present the incident through rose-coloured glasses.

The Inquest

The inquest was conducted the day after James' death – on Sunday 6 January, 1864, in the District Court of Clunes. The Presiding Magistrate was Coroner WILLIAM BAXTER LEES.

The witnesses were:

JOHN TRIMBLE ROBINSON (doctor)

PATRICK THURAN (constable)

CATHERINE KIRBY (wife)

JOHN KIRBY (son)

JOHN RAYNES (carter)

JOHN HAWKINS and JOHN JONES (carters)

6 January, 1864 – B. LEES Coroner

The deceased James Kirby was found on the Talbot Road near Clunes dead on the sixth day of January 1864. I was of the opinion that the deceased died on the sixth instant from internal injuries caused by a bullock dray passing over his body.

William Baxter Lees

CORONER WILLIAM BAXTER LEES conducted the inquest in the South Clunes courthouse on 6 January 1864, the day after James' death. Basing his conclusions on the evidence of the rather forthright John Raynes at whose house the drinking spree occurred, the coroner mistakenly stated that James died on Sunday morning. This does not match up with the evidence provided by everyone else, including Doctor Robinson and James' drinking partners, John Hawkins and John Jones. These two Johns had left him near their homes on Mount Beckworth Road at 7.00 o'clock, Saturday night. James was run over by his own dray ten minutes later, a further half mile up the road.

It is a mystery why the coroner chose to accept Raynes's version rather than the Hawkins and Jones version. Maybe Raynes thought that James had died on the morning of the fifth because the body seemed to be still warm, which can be explained by the effect of the hot summer sun. It is an indisputable fact that James met his death the previous night after he had left Raynes' house on the evening of the fifth, not on the morning of the sixth as stated by the coroner. When a person is almost cut in half by an unforgiving wagon wheel, death is immediate. Even people in high places are fallible.

It was just after Christmas and the height of summer in a hot part of Victoria. Refrigeration did not exist. Burials had to take place as quickly as possible – within twenty-four hours. James was buried on that same Sunday, 6 January, at Clunes Cemetery. His grave, according to the cemetery trustee, Margaret McFarlane, is Catholic Section B1, Grave 63, close to the fence and under a tree.

(1) DEPOSITION OF WITNESS – JOHN TRIMBLE ROBINSON

> *I am a legally qualified medical practitioner residing in Clunes. I have*
> *this day made a post mortem examination of the body of the deceased.*
> *Externally I found a slight abrasion of the skin over the left hip, a*
> *slight wound of the face and little finger of the left hand.*

*On removing the skin from the lower part of the left side I observed
some black effused blood and found three floating ribs fractured on
the same side. In cutting into the abdomen I found a large quantity
of effused black blood, which had proceeded from the spleen, which
was completely torn in two parts, each part having a large quantity
of blood attached to it. One of the floating ribs on the right side was
also fractured, and the convex fraction of the right side of the liver
was slightly torn. I examined the brain. I consider the deceased died
from rupture of the spleen and effusion of blood into the cavity of the
abdomen. A bullock dray wheel would be likely to cause such injuries as
the deceased had. I believe the deceased died immediately after receiving
the injury* [making Raynes' version of events unlikely]. *The
deceased was fully fifty years old.* [Catherine thought he was 38.]
J. T. Robinson

*6 January 1864 – South Clunes before coroner (District of Creswick)
Before W. B. Lees, Coroner*

DOCTOR JOHN TRIMBLE ROBINSON examined the body in the
morning of 6 January. As a medical practitioner, he focused on medical
issues: three broken ribs, black blood from the spleen – torn into two
parts, three broken ribs including one fractured floating rib, damage to
the arm and face. It appeared that James had been virtually cut in half by
the savage impact of the bullock dray wheel, but that most of the damage
had been concealed under his clothing.

(2) DEPOSITION OF WITNESS – PATRICK THURAN

*I am a constable stationed at Clunes. I received information this
morning at seven o'clock that deceased was lying on the road dead.
I found deceased lying on the road about three quarters of a mile
from Clunes. I examined the place and found the marks of the wheels
near where the deceased lay, the grooves which was dusty was much
disturbed from the place where the deceased lay about six feet off.*

*I found no marks on the body but the left hand was much injured. I
have been in charge of the body of the deceased ever since.
I searched the person of deceased and found an empty purse, a knife, a
pipe and a match box.
Deceased is not known to me.
Patrick Thuran*

*Taken and sworn before me the sixth day of January A.D. 1864 at
South Clunes
Before W. B. Lees – Coroner*

CONSTABLE PATRICK THURAN had his own version of the incident. He may have been an excellent policeman but his English is less
than perfect. As a representative of the law he was more interested in
the attendant circumstances rather medical issues, which he left to the
doctor. He described the incident as happening three quarters of a mile
from Clunes, his version differing from the two miles alluded to by the
other witnesses. Maybe he was referring to the outskirts rather than the
centre. According to him, the only sign of injury was on the left hand,
and he didn't see any marks on the body. What he did notice, being the
typical policeman, was the empty purse, the knife, a pipe and a match-
box.

(3) DEPOSITION OF WITNESS – CATHERINE KIRBY

*I am the wife of the deceased. I last saw deceased at half past seven on
Saturday morning. Deceased left me to go for a load of wood. He had
a dray with eight bullocks. He was in good health and perfectly sober. I
thought deceased would be back about five or six o'clock in the evening.
I went out at about five o'clock to meet deceased coming home. I came
home again in half an hour when I saw nothing of deceased. The
bullocks and dray that deceased took with him on yesterday morning
came home last night before I went out looking for deceased. There
was no one driving the bullocks and dray and we could find no trace*

of the deceased until this morning about seven o'clock. I sent my son John this morning to look for deceased. He returned about an hour after stating deceased was lying on telegraph road with his eyes open and he thought dead.

I went to Mr McDonald and others and told them of it. They then went with me. We saw deceased lying about three quarters of a mile from our house. He was quite dead. Mr McDonald got a cart to bring deceased to Mrs Edmundson's where the body now lies. Deceased was of temperate habits. [As his wife, Cathy chose to carefully embroider the facts – 'temperate' is open to interpretation.] *Deceased was accustomed to the bullocks. They were perfectly quiet when they came home.*

I was married to deceased eleven and a half years ago. My maiden name is Catherine McLaughlan. [Cathy used the 'O' and the 'Mc' versions interchangeably.] *I don't know the names of the deceased's parents.* [James was quite secretive about his past.] *Deceased was born in Cork Ireland. Deceased was a short time in Sydney and has been about twenty years in Victoria.*

I have seven children by deceased. I now have only one boy alive and five girls. Deceased was thirty-eight years old. [Forty-one according to ancestry.com, but 'fully fifty years old' according to the coroner.] *I never knew of deceased having a fit. I have resided about two miles from here with deceased. Deceased had no money when deceased left me on yesterday morning. I don't believe he got any money yesterday.'*

Catherine **X** *Kirby*

Taken and sworn by me sixth day January AD 1864.

W. B. Lees – Coroner

Cathy probably remembers such intimate details as James attacking voraciously that last hearty breakfast of bacon and eggs, and the customary, romantic, farewell smooch, the jangle of the harness, the crack of the whip, the 'Giddyup – move it', the crunch of hooves on gravel … and suddenly they're away. But this is not the stuff of inquests.

For the inquest, Cathy's first memory was James' 7.30 am departure. How did she know the time, as she almost certainly didn't have a clock? Probably she just guessed from the position of the summer sun. What is most important is that she confirmed that James had a dray with eight bullocks and that she expected him back at five or six o'clock .

It is obvious that Cathy's testimony has been severely edited. One cannot imagine the above clinical voice to be that of Catherine Kirby. This calm passionless statement of events had to be a version written by the court scribe.

It seems that James was either ignorant of his origins, or more likely that he was quite secretive in what he chose to share with Cathy. It appears that he pretended to be much younger than he actually was.

(4) DEPOSITION OF WITNESS – JOHN KIRBY

The deceased is my father. I don't know my age. [Born 11 May 1853 – therefore he is ten years of age at this time.] *I don't know what it is to take an oath. I have never heard the Bible read. I went out with my father the deceased yesterday morning to get a load of wood. We went out about three miles. I saw my father load the wood with the assistance of James Ryan. Ryan left some time before me. Ryan was quite sober yesterday and so was deceased. I did not hear any quarrelling between deceased and Ryan. It was about two o'clock on yesterday when I got home. My mother sent me this morning to look for deceased. I found deceased lying on the telegraph road dead. I then ran home. I told my mother. I then went back with my mother and then I showed her where deceased was lying. I saw the bullocks come home last night. It was just dark when I got the bullocks out.*
John <u>X</u> Kirby

[His mark. Could John read and write? Did he attend school? Probably not. Was he simply too young to handle a deposition? Surely he could at least sign his name, or does he stubbornly refuse to learn – like his mum?]

Taken and sworn by me sixth day January AD 1864.
W.B.Lees – Coroner

JOHN KIRBY, as we already know, was ten years old. Summing up, he didn't know his own age or his father's age, had never been to school, couldn't read or write, had never heard the Bible read, and didn't know what it meant to take an oath. What he did know was that on that fateful day he had gone out three miles along the Clunes-Talbot Road with his dad and James Ryan for a load of wood. He arrived home at 2.00 o'clock, leaving his father at the hotel with his three mates. James did not come home that night. Cathy assumed that he was over the limit and had stayed the night with John Raynes rather than risk her wrath. The following morning at 7.00 o'clock she sent John to find him. John was devastated when he found James lying on the Telegraph Road dead. He ran home and informed his mother, and they both ran back to where James was still lying. John affirmed that it was dark when the bullocks came home, but he was adept enough to release the bullocks from the dray and provide them with feed for the night.

(5) DEPOSITION OF WITNESS – JOHN RAYNES

I am a carter residing at the junction two miles from Clunes. I have
known deceased the last three years. I believe the last time I saw
deceased was on Sunday last. Mr McDonald came home this morning
and told me deceased was lying dead on the road. I went with him and
another man and the wife and son of the deceased. I got to the body
first and found him on the road dead. Deceased was lying on his back
his hands on his side and his knees partly raised from the ground.
I then gave information to the police. I came back with the police and

I saw the body removed to where it now lies. I have frequently seen deceased the worse of liquor but not this last winter. [How about this summer?]
I saw no marks on the clothes of the deceased. I observed a slight mark on his left side and his left hand severely cut. I believed he had been dead about an hour before I saw him this morning. He was quite warm when I first saw him.

John Raynes

Taken and sworn before me the sixth day of January A.D. 1864 at South Clunes.

W. B. Lees – Coroner

JOHN RAYNES lived at the junction of the Clunes-Ballarat and Mount Beckworth Roads, two miles from Clunes properly so-called. It was at his house that the four mates had spent Saturday afternoon drinking. When John heard the news he rushed to the spot where James was discovered. Sunday was a hot day and on finding the body warm under the morning sun, John Raynes expressed the view that James must have died within the last hour on Sunday morning. No one else appeared to agree with this version of events except the coroner who may have been influenced by Raynes's assertive personality.

(6) DEPOSITION OF WITNESS – JOHN HAWKINS

I am a carter residing near Clunes. I have known deceased for the last five years. I last saw deceased alive last night about seven o'clock. I had then just left this house with deceased. [Note that the deposition took place at his house, not at the court-house.] *I left him about a half a mile from here.* [The body was three quarters of a mile from the house according to John, ten minutes away from where John Hawkins and John Jones had left him after the three of them had walked together for half a mile from John Raynes' house at the junction. The ten minutes may have been a half a mile. This would suggest that the distance from Raynes' house to James' house was about one and three quarter miles.] *He went across the range* [Presumably this was the hilly road towards Mount Beckworth where he lived and where he hoped to catch up with the oxen.] *John Jones went home from there and I went straight on my way too. I only saw deceased drink ale and ginger beer at this house. I was perfectly sober and so was John Jones on last night* [obviously not wishing to be blamed for the events that followed]. *When we left this house with deceased, deceased was a little merry but perfectly capable of taking care of himself.* [But was he over .05?] *When deceased left us last night, his bullocks were a good bit ahead of him. Deceased ran after them as he left us. From the place where deceased was found, I believe deceased must have fallen about ten minutes after leaving Jones and myself last night. I have never seen deceased drunk all last winter.* [But how about on a hot, thirsty, January day after a hard morning's work cutting and loading timber? They had been drinking for about four hours as good mates do. They are under oath and therefore careful not to lie. 'Last winter' may be a red herring.]

John Hawkins

Taken and sworn before me the sixth day of January A.D. 1864 at South Clunes

W. B. Lees – Coroner

JOHN HAWKINS and JOHN JONES, James' two other drinking partners, fellow timber carters, both lived half a mile along Mount Beckworth Road. John Hawkins declared that James had drunk a moderate mix of beer and ginger ale. He asserted that they had not seen James drunk for over six months. The word 'drunk' is rather fluid in its interpretation. The quantity actually imbibed of James' life-sustaining fluid is open to question. John Hawkins is under oath and chooses his words carefully so as not to lie. Be that as it may, James had left them at a run at about eight o'clock in an effort to catch up with his recalcitrant bullocks.

Ten minutes later, we have the probable scenario. A further mile down the road, James sees bullocks and dray in the gathering darkness. He shouts to them in vain, 'Whoa there!' and a few other expletives. Because of the wheels rumbling in the gravel and the loud shuffling of hooves, they pay no attention. James, still not too steady on his feet after the afternoon's activities, attempts the supremely risky manoeuvre of running in front of the front wheel in an attempt to clamber on to the dray. Normally you mount a dray when it's stationary. He slips. He falls crossways in the path of an unforgiving ironclad wheel. It would have been a painless death. It was all over within seconds.

REQUIESCAT IN PACE

A Woodcutter's Funeral

Cathy gathered together her brood, and they all wept unrestrainedly. For Cathy, it was the loss of her partner, her lover and the family breadwinner.

For the children, they understood death in different ways. For John, his father James was more than 'Da' or 'Dad'; he was his teacher, his boss, his role model and his best friend. For the girls he provided cuddles every morning before he went off on the dray, and the same every night when he walked or staggered in the door. He bought them things, like dolls and food; he made them things like that box that he turned into a doll's house. There was that hollow feeling when they stared at the empty chair – Dad's special chair at the head of the table. Gut-wrenching sadness pervaded the house.

The day of the funeral was a nightmare for all. It happened on the Monday, two days after James' death, for obvious practical reasons. It was the height of summer. There was no refrigeration. Blowflies were buzzing and maggots were ready to infest. The funeral had to happen that day at the latest, early morning, Monday 7 January. Cathy was in no state to organise a funeral. James' mates, the three Johns – John Hawkins, John Jones and John Raynes – knocked up a primitive coffin from the lumber that James had stashed under the house. It was obvious why they had chosen to be wood carters rather than carpenters.

Cathy's and John's statements at the coroner's inquest had been severely edited for the sake of legal requirements. They were both shell-shocked, and they fought valiantly to control their inner turmoil in the presence of the magistrate. But once back home it was a different story. Grief repressed has a way of suddenly exploding uncontrollably. By the Monday of the funeral, Cathy was an emotional mess. She tried to repress her tears to spare the children. But she fell apart, a prey to guilt and despair. She was like a runaway train. Why ever did she begrudge James a drink or two after a hard day's work? Yet it was the drink that assuredly led to his death! John, now supposedly the man of the house, was just a little boy who had lost his da – his idol, his mate, his mentor. The whole family clung to each other and wailed with unstinting abandon. Six-month-old Ellen, who knew nothing about death, joined with the others, sobbing uncomprehendingly.

How could Cathy get herself sufficiently under control to organise a funeral? Fortunately John Hawkins, one of the three Johns and faithful drinking partner, offered his services. He sent a message by Cobb and Co coach to Creswick requesting the services of Father John McGirr, Parish Priest of St Augustine's, for a funeral at short notice. McGirr, a dedicated Irish pastor, was always ready to serve his flock, particularly when they had strayed and needed a hand in getting to the other side. He saw James as a fitting candidate for his pastoral zeal. Whether they were churchgoers or not made no difference to John McGirr. If they were Irish, they already had a foot in the door. In fact, they were 'in like Flynn' – Flynn being an Irishman 'to be sure, to be sure, to be sure.' So the good Father McGirr walked out the door at 7.00 am, mounted his trusty nag and made the fourteen miles from Creswick to Clunes in three hours, arriving just in time for the 10.00 o'clock funeral.

The funeral service took place in the new Clunes wooden chapel, the forerunner to the bluestone church of Saint Thomas Aquinas. All of James' friends and acquaintances were there, plus a bevy of grateful, tried and true customers. Cathy and the children had already shed their tears and now stood with heads bowed in distraught silence for the ceremony. Their grief emerged again as the coffin was lowered into the unforgiving hole in the ground at the Clunes Cemetery. Father McGirr intoned the words, 'O God, we commit the mortal remains of your servant James to your fond embrace. Earth to earth. Dust to dust . . . ' It was all too much for what was left of the Kirby family. Once again their grief took over.

> *One hundred and fifty-five years later, Margaret Walshe, Margaret Vrkljan and Peter Hall gathered at the Clunes Cemetery to lay a tombstone above the remains of our great-great-grandfather, James Kirby. Discovering the site of what was an unmarked grave was a challenge, particularly as it was covered in undergrowth and trees, the last gravesite at the end of a line and engulfed by bushes. At the time of his death, Catherine and family were short of funds for such luxuries as tombstones. She would have marked the site with a simple wooden cross, which with the ravages of time was swallowed up by the encroaching bush. But we, her progeny would not let it go. With a little bit of research we found the site. Our seven generations had their origins in the Cathy and James Kirby story. Long live their memory!*

Kindly neighbours popped in every day. At least here was food on the table. But the coffers were bare, as were James' pockets at the time of his demise. Death in the goldfields was a common occurrence, whether caused by mine cave-ins, explosions, rock-falls, or human miscalculation. To this you add the effects of liquor and of various illnesses in an age of primitive medicine. Cathy knew about death. But she thought that disaster and death were things of the past. It happened to others, but, touch wood, not to her and hers. She had felt secure with James, her faithful husband, despite his appetite for the amber fluid. She had looked confidently towards a prosperous future and revelled in the security of her family unit. But now all she could see was hopelessness and devastation and penury. But at least she had her six beautiful children.

It took a month for her to regain possession of herself.

'Think positive, girl!' she repeated endlessly. 'Where there's life, there's hope! The McLaughlans never give up! Nor do the Kirbys!'

Money was a serious issue. How can a widow and six children survive without an income? With six young children, and no other family to assist with child-minding, there was no way of working for a living. There were no government handouts in those days. There was a limit to the largesse of generous neighbours. Cathy had to stand on her own two feet.

'Come on, girl. Think!'

Cathy was still young at thirty. She was passably easy on the eye. There were many miners looking for female companionship, and they were prepared to pay for it. But for Cathy it was a last resort. There had to be a better way. What would James advise? Despite his attraction for the demon drink, he had been a loyal husband totally committed to her and the kids.

'So, girl, think.'

Hiring out her body would be the last resort. But not beyond the realm of possibility!

The first step in reinventing herself was the difficult decision to sell the bullocks and dray. It was like tearing out her heart. It was James' livelihood and his heart and soul. But when she thought about it, it became such a logical step to take. But also maybe a slightly vindictive thing to do! Indeed she blamed their bullocks and dray, as well as the hostelry establishment, that other Bullock and Dray, for James' death. Cathy asked around. None of the mates had ready cash or the need for such a purchase. She might get six pound each for the bullocks and another fifty for the dray at the Clunes market. So Cathy had a sign made up by James' mate, John Raynes, who could read and write. So three weeks later, Catherine set off for the Clunes market with eight bullocks and dray for sale:

• DRAY AND EIGHT BULLOCKS – 150 pounds •

A prospective bullocky beat her down to one hundred and ten pounds. He only wanted six of the oxen because he already had two of his own. It was a reasonable deal, and Cathy had no option but to accept. In fact, it was better than she had calculated because at that time there was a considerable fluctuation in the market. She was on the way back. The five-acre block provided sufficient fodder for her two remaining oxen, Bullo and Boris.

The next challenge was to find a good man who was prepared to take on a second-hand wife and six kids. The bargaining chip was having the house thrown in, not to mention two healthy but out-of-condition bullocks. Living accommodation consisted of an attractive, solid, spacious, well-constructed log cabin set in the foothills of Mount Beckworth. It looked quite good on paper despite the few outstanding debts.

The kids were growing up fast. Ellen was now six months. Annie was the typical two-year-old, running around the house throwing tantrums. Elizabeth at four, mummy's helper, all too often was seen on her knees crying over spilt milk and other childhood disasters. The gentle one, Margaret, now six, would sit on James' chair and suck her thumb, occasionally bursting into tears and wailing, 'I want my dad!'

Little happy-go-lucky Catherine at nine swallowed her tears and her sadness and tried to put on the same forced smile as her mum Catherine. John, now the ten-year-old man-of-the-house, continued to gather kindling, chop wood, tend the fire, fetch water from the creek and tend the bullocks. The kids were a welcome distraction over those first three devastating weeks. When the six bullocks and dray were led away to be sold at the market, once again John was a prey to that same gut-wrenching sadness, akin to what he experienced at the loss of his dad and best mate. He wandered into the bush all alone and howled unrestrainedly.

The next thing to go would be the house. James' creditors had displayed a certain degree of patience. But at the end of twelve months they began to call in their debts. Cathy was desperate to find another breadwinner. She was quite at her wits' end. She had a theory about love. If she could find a generous, hard-working man, she would mould him into a man she could love.

11

Cathy Gets Her Man

There was indeed light at the end of the tunnel. Twelve months later that generous, hard-working man materialised. His name was George Lawson. He was a small-time farmer. The sticking point was that he happened to be, of all things, a *Protestant.*

How was the connection initiated? It so happened that Margy Staunton was the catalyst responsible for the chemistry that followed. Knowing that Cathy was the archetypal, malleable, potato famine girl, Margy, a mutual Mount Beckworth friend, used an essentially female ploy to arrange for a meeting between George and Cathy. Margy was an experienced matchmaker and had three or four success stories to her credit. Here she had a widow seeking a new husband. The house was on the market. Margy knew about farmer George, who was short of cash and a wife, and who grew potatoes. Just maybe this might be a match made in heaven. Out of curiosity, George fell for the bait, as did Cathy.

Cathy, with her bubbly personality plus a house for sale, looked like an attractive deal. But a widow with six kids? How could this reclusive Protestant bachelor cope with an Irish Catholic widow with six kids? But when he met the kids and saw the solid, largely paid-for log cabin, he thought this was a deal worthy of serious consideration. George was usually slow to make up his mind, being essentially cautious about the big decisions in life. But exuberant Cathy, with her six delightful kids, all on their best behaviour, and a house thrown in for good measure, defeated his reluctance to make a decision on the hop. He would think about it. Seriously!

Young George was born in 1825. George's parents, William and Deborah Lawson, had named him after the popular King of England, George IV, who reigned from 1820 to 1830. They were simple working class people but ardent monarchists. So it was obvious why they chose to name their son after their revered monarch.

William was a labourer but he wanted the best for his oldest son George. They lived in Buckinghamshire, between Oxford and London. William and Deborah, despite their humble background, tried to inculcate a little class into George. Hence George's somewhat posh accent. They lived close to Aylesbury Grammar School, which was a well-regarded educational institution, where one studied the Classics and, of course, Shakespeare. George's best friend Clive went to Aylesbury Grammar. Clive was quite adept at spouting out: *'amo, amas, amat ...'* and reciting 'Friends, Romans, countrymen, lend me your ears.'

George was never too sure why they didn't just say something like, 'Listen up, you lot!'

But he was impressed enough to retain it for use at the right time. The best William and Deborah could afford for their son George was Grade 8 at the local primary school. Clive spoke with a plum-in-the-mouth upper-crust accent, and George, being quite intelligent and eager to learn, latched on to such key words as 'smashing', 'by golly', 'cheers', 'jolly good' and 'simply marvellous'. For better or worse, George subsequently brought this lingo to Australia, which made him the perfect subject for teasing, a skill that Aussies had down to a fine art.

When George Lawson was in his twenties, his father William died suddenly of a heart attack, and the family fell on hard times. Young George, hearing about the gold rush in Australia, made the momentous decision to seek his fortune on the Australian goldfields. He emptied his piggy bank and off he went to Australia to seek his fortune.

Like so many others, George did not manage to strike gold. So, as he had already demonstrated his skill at digging, he decided on a new occupation that involved digging – that of farmer. Despite his English-style education, George was not a snob, nor an academic. He had a special affinity for life on the land. For several years, he scrabbled and scraped to make a living selling produce to miners. His specialty was potatoes. The Chinese market gardeners had taken over the fruit and vegetable market, and large landowners had commandeered the grain market. But George saw potatoes, easy and cheap to grow, as a potential source of income. He really wanted to diversify and be the master of his own slice of rural land. The question was how to achieve this dream. Maybe he now had a viable option.

George was a shy man who could not compete with the glib-tongued Irishmen and the other European racial mix that surrounded him. Maybe Cathy was the answer. If he was honest with himself, he felt quite out of place. He was seven years older than Cathy. George told Cathy about the small property he had leased in the foothills of Mount Beckworth where he was trying to grow, of all things, *potatoes*. What a coincidence! Cathy had a special place in her heart for the humble potato.

Encouraged by Cathy's positive reaction, George decided to share with her his ultimate dream. He had his eye on a thirty-acre block five miles south of Talbot and to the east of Stoney Creek. Most prospective buyers saw it as an unattractive proposition because of its relatively dry, stony soil. And for good measure, it was pock-holed with three abandoned mineshafts and heaps of tailings. The asking price was quite reasonable as the owners were desperate to sell.

George saw its possibilities. It was not far from Stoney Creek, which was a tributary of Back Creek, the main water source for Clunes. Stoney Creek was fed by a few surrounding dry-bed creeks that flowed when there was rain. George reasoned that, if he blocked off one of the dry creeks that ran through this property, he could create a dam that would fill up whenever there was heavy rainfall. Thus he could turn this unproductive land into a viable proposition. Cathy was impressed by George's creative thinking, which might overcome their limited budget

Better still, this Stoney Creek property came with a little tin-roofed cottage. Not far from the cottage there were sundry hillocks and depressions as well as mineshafts left by disappointed gold-miners. Maybe they could use these holes in the ground creatively. The abandoned mineshafts could give them a second water-storage option. Surely it would be possible to channel water from the creek bed during rainy seasons to the mineshaft area. The soil on the low side of the mineshafts had a tinge of green about it, the result of seepage from the shafts during the rainy season. George's enthusiasm was contagious. Cathy was beginning to fall in love not only with George – yes – but even more so with his capacity for creative thinking.

The Stoney Creek property was five miles south of Clunes and twelve miles north of Mount Beckworth – a half a day's walk. No problem! But before this prospective farming property could prove productive, the water plan would have to be implemented. That would take at least a year. How to live in the meantime? On the positive side, George's ambition was to run twenty cattle and plant more potatoes and maybe parsnips, carrots, cabbages or whatever the market suggested at that time. But none of this could happen before they had sorted out the water problem, which would cost time and money. George, a farm labourer, could barely scrape up a living at the only occupation that matched his budget and his capabilities. He needed capital to realise his dream. Cathy was assuredly the answer …

But there was one significant problem. The said George Lawson wasn't a Catholic. Nor was he Irish. In fact, he was a dyed-in-the-wool Protestant, born in Buckinghamshire. That made him English – a member of the race that was responsible for the deaths of Cathy's family during the Potato Famine. On the other hand, he was tall, dark and handsome, shy, good-humoured and had a delightfully winning smile. Being born close to Oxford, he spoke with what Cathy thought was a posh English accent. 'We could do with a bit of class in the Kirby family', said Cathy to herself. There was nothing wrong with being upwardly mobile. Was there any chance that such a match could work?

'As for not bein' a Catholic', Cathy mused, 'maybe he'll convert. I must admit that I 'aven't seen the inside of a church since the funeral. Just 'ow important is religion to me?' Food for thought!

Cathy had some serious thinking to do. For sure, George was ambitious, hardworking, passably good-looking. And, yes, he had shared with her his dream about the possible property deal at Stoney Creek. Yes, it was within reach of the town of Back Creek, or Talbot, as it was now called. Yes, this man trusted her. George had suddenly let go of his characteristic reticence. But maybe it was just a bit of manipulation. He wanted her money so that he could buy his dream piece of real estate. But wasn't she doing the same sort of thing – using him to play the role of man-of-the-house and provide her family with on-going security and food on the table and be a father-figure for her children and a man to share her bed?

A plan formed in her mind. A deal could be possible. The musing continued:

'I'm a widow with six kids, I have a few debts, but I have a house to sell. George doesn't even have enough for a deposit for this chunk of dry, stony land. I think I have the upper hand. Yes, I'm sure we can make a deal!'

The children, particularly John, just wanted their dad back. They weren't too sure about this other bloke. But when they met George, his gentle, friendly manner and his quirky sense of humour slowly won them over. He wasn't as good as their real dad but maybe he would do. Just maybe!

So a deal was struck – a new man in the house, food on the table, life on a farm, a chance for a new life, and, for Cathy, a brand-new sleeping companion. It's possible they would all learn to smile again. Who knew what the future would bring?

The deal covered finance, property, a farmhouse, two bullocks, settlement of debts, work, and responsibility for the children. Both Cathy and George agreed on the essentials. They would put Cathy's present home on the market. James' ghost still hovered around the house, which was mostly James' handiwork. James would be remembered and loved forever, but they all needed a new start – Cathy, George and the six children. They would sell the house that James had built, they would combine whatever funds they could raise, and they would invest in the new Stoney Creek property. And the proactive Cathy declared:

'And to celebrate the deal, let's get married!'

It all looked so perfect. But there was one sticking point. Cathy did not want to marry in a Protestant church. And George 'as sure as hell' didn't want to marry in a Roman Catholic church. Cathy assured him in no uncertain terms:

'I am not a Roman Catholic. I'm an Irish Catholic. St Francis' Church, where me and my last 'usband got married is a not a *Roman* Catholic Church. It's an *Australian* Catholic church!'

George's response was simply, 'It's the same thing! Let's not split hairs!'

Cathy's Irish temper flared up. 'It's not the same thing. I'm a Catholic through and through. I don't know much, but I do know that you Proddies were once Catholics till Henry VIII did the dirty on us. 'e was a wife-killer and 'e invented his own new church.'

George responded vehemently: 'The Roman church was rotten to the core from the Pope down. We Anglicans came along and reformed it!'

John blocked his ears and shouted: 'Cut it out, you grown-ups! Who cares about churches? Just let's be happy!'

Young Catherine began to cry. 'You're making me sad again!'

The other girls, Margy, Lizzy, Annie and Ellen, likewise burst into tears on cue. George suddenly cooled down and settled the kids down,

'OK children! I'm sorry! Catherine, I apologise. Give me a hug. I don't know what got into me!'

Cathy responded: 'OK! Let's not fight about churches.' And added wisely, 'There's good and bad in all of 'em.'

'Right,' said George. 'For the moment, we'll just live together and pool our resources. I'll earn the money and pay the bills. You'll look after the kids. Deal?'

'OK!' responded Cathy, 'But gettin' married properly is still on the cards! We'll sort it out later.'

And that's what they did – much later!

Stoney Creek

They said their goodbyes to the neighbours, settled outstanding debts, cleared out the log cabin of their furniture and possessions, and stacked all of their goods on a borrowed jinker. George, John and their two mates, John Raynes and John Hawkins, did the loading. They still had their two oxen, Bullo and Boris, to pull the heavy load. Later that morning they left Mount Beckworth behind and set out for Stoney Creek. It took them the rest of the day to cover the twelve miles to their new abode and an hour to unload the jinker. That night George, John and the two mates bunked down at the Stoney Creek cottage. They were on the trail back to Mount Beckworth at dawn for the second load. After loading up, the three Johns shook hands. Young John, who saw himself man of the house after George, thanked James' good mates with the earnestness of a ten-year-old, and assured them that he and George could manage the rest themselves.

Cathy and the kids had completed the final cleanup and would have handed over the keys to the new owners if they'd had any. Keys were something that they never worried about at Mount Beckworth! They said their *final* goodbyes to the neighbours and hit the road once again late afternoon for Stoney Creek. The two bullocks were at the end of their tether, in both senses. The passage of years and the carting of hundreds of tons of logs had taken their toll. The jinker groaned under the load of George, Cathy and the six kids, crammed together with the remaining jumble of furniture and household bibs and bobs. The weather was balmy. Thankfully, no mozzies! They were all thoroughly exhausted. So after an uncomfortable eight miles, they crashed where they were – beside the road, surrounded by bush – and there they slept like the proverbial logs.

The following day, they were up with the cockatoos. Three hours later they had reached their destination, a mere twelve miles to the north of Mount Beckworth. The first thing the kids did was rush to explore their new home. 'First in, first served', they yelled as they charged in, bent on 'bagsing their pozzies' in the bedrooms. As a family of six they lived by that mantra, despite Cathy's admonitions to the contrary. But the voice of authority finally settled them down. They agreed that it was a bit 'squashy'! So the girls got the big room. John was happy to sleep in the junk room, while the good room looking out on to the paddocks and the mine tailings was perfect for Cathy and her new paramour. After a practice run they both agreed that it was a thoroughly workable arrangement.

It took twelve months for Cathy, George and the six children to settle in. They all had their allotted tasks. The first challenge was to stay healthy and keep on breathing, which they managed to do quite well. They were essentially a healthy lot!

The second challenge was to ensure a reliable water source for the home. Fortunately their dwelling was equipped with a five hundred gallon rainwater tank. Given that the annual rainfall was rarely above twenty inches and that their tank water was essentially for drinking and cooking, personal ablutions were minimal. The weekly bath was conducted with a quarter of a bucket of their precious water and a face-washer, the latter being used for more than their faces – more specifically to sponge themselves down from top to toe. Whenever it rained, they would doff their gear, run in all directions with their smidgeon of soap, and luxuriate in the pleasure of being marginally clean.

The third challenge was to develop a reliable water source for the farm. Cathy was fixated on a commercially viable vegie garden. To achieve this dream they would need an abundance of water. George agreed to factor Cathy's dream into their master plan. Their first priority was to create a dam. This meant constructing a dam wall that would capture the water that occasionally flowed in the dry creek at the top of their property. They chose a narrow section of the creek-bed for the dam wall. Their immediate task was to wedge in boulders and rocks to block off the gap, with clay to fill in the spaces between. The plan was to create a six-foot wall sloping downhill that would withstand the body of water that would hopefully eventuate. George calculated that he would lose fifty per cent of water stored through seepage and evaporation. Their dam would be about one hundred and twenty yards long and twenty wide at its widest part. This should be enough for their immediate needs. As a backup, George planned to channel the overflow into the abandoned mineshafts just below the house. To access this water, he would have to locate the vegie garden close to the dam and the mineshafts. To transport the water to the vegie patch, they would have to form a bucket brigade, or better still, when they could afford it, some kind of pumping system.

George was so proud of himself. What an ingenious solution for their water problem! At the Clunes gold mines they had steam-activated pumps. There was no way he could afford that. How about a windmill? Distinctly possible! But windmills are too slow. Yes, but if they are operating day and night, he could pump water from the mineshafts to a header tank or directly on to the garden. He secretly said to himself, 'Maybe I should have been an engineer!'

The family, including three-year-old Sarah, worked tirelessly, filling buckets with pebbles and stones from the proposed garden site and transporting them to the growing dam wall. One month later, they had managed to buy for a nominal sum a small, rickety, second-hand ox cart and yoke from neighbour Cyril Soames. Bullo and Boris, despite the passage of years, were still invaluable, dragging round cartloads of rock and stones in the old cart that jounced its way over the rubble. They worked on all three projects simultaneously – the construction of the dam, the diversion of the lower part of the creek towards the mineshafts, and the establishment of the market garden. They sifted soil, removed stones and dug in weeds and dry grass for the proposed garden site. Bullo and Boris made their special contribution to the fertility of the soil in a predictable way and in a manner in which cattle are particularly adept.

It is now winter of 1866. They have been working tirelessly on their three projects. The winter rains began to fall on cue. Their dry creek was no longer dry. They soon discovered that the gravelly base of their dam had an insatiable thirst for water that immediately disappeared into the subsoil just as George had predicted. 'OK, everyone! Patience! We have to wait till the dam bottom becomes totally waterlogged.' They thought George was swearing. Then came their first spelling lesson: 'd-a-m is different from d-a-m-n.' They all nodded their heads, sagely, but inwardly they weren't so sure.

One month later the level of the muddy water began to rise – inexorably. But as soon as the dam began to fill, within a few days their stock of water disappeared into the dry soil. As George predicted, it took months for the clayey soil to become super-saturated enabling them to create a reasonable water reserve. They were winning, but ever so slowly.

Their prime source of revenue was to be their market garden. Cyril Soames had a rusty old ploughshare from the days when he had tried to grow lucerne for his cattle. He had since given up on both the lucerne and the ploughshare. He generously bequeathed the latter to George.

'Georgie m' boy, it's all yours. When yer dig up yer first spuds, yer might spare one or two fer me and the missus!'

Bullo and Boris took it in turns to drag the ploughshare around the first acre allocated to the garden beds. They cleared away most of the stones, ploughed what they now called soil to a depth of one foot, and mixed in decaying vegetable matter from beneath the trees at the bottom of the property. They still needed to add some kind of fertiliser to the mix.

During their first year at Stoney Creek, they had got to know quite a few of their neighbours. The Kirby kids were the draw-card.

'No hissy-fits, hardworking and positive – a credit to their parents!' There was a bit of talk about the different surnames, but they decided it was none of their business.

'They're a great family, hardworking, friendly, ready to help out when needed. That's all we need to know!' declared Cyril Soames to good neighbour Marjorie Blake over the barbedwire fence. Marjorie thoroughly agreed.

'Them kids is treasures, and although the wife would never win a beauty contest she works like a beaver, and she done such a good job on them girls. And young John, I could hug 'im to death. And as fer the pommy bloke, e's absolutely gorrrgeous!'

Cyril Soames had a large property of seventy acres. He ran fifty beef cattle. He was fascinated by George and Cathy's master plan. No one thought that a dry former mine site could ever be productive. When he saw what they had achieved in six months, particularly their water conservation plan, he was absolutely flabbergasted. Cyril was ready to make a serious contribution – a year's worth of cattle dung for their proposed market garden.

13

'Be Fruitful and Multiply'

T hen, surprise, surprise! In May 1866, Cathy began to experience the familiar symptoms. 'Jesus!' she said, not expecting another one just yet, just when they were trying to get themselves established. As for George, he was over the moon. Cathy was thirty-three years old. Was she praying or cursing? Probably a little of each! But when she thought about it, she decided that she had reason to be overjoyed. In fact she couldn't wipe the smile off her face. When she told George, at first he was speechless, totally gobsmacked, and then, uncharacteristically, he let out a wild whoop. Cathy shushed him.

'Take it easy, Georgie dear! Keep it between ourselves till we are absolutely sure.'

So George with great difficulty buttoned his lip as well as his emotions. For the moment!

True to her word, Cathy kept the news under wraps. She didn't want to distract the family from their work on the water and garden projects. And she certainly didn't want the family nagging at her:

'Take it easy, ma!'

'Time for a rest!'

'Think of the baby!'

She knew everything there was to know about babies. She didn't want advice from the kids or anyone else including George. George with difficulty kept his mouth shut and his emotions under wraps. It was 'keep mum' for the moment – in fact 'keep mum on the job!'

Eleven-year-old Catherine was the first one to twig.

'Ma, you're getting a bit fat, aren't you,' she declared one evening, with a wink to the others. 'What's going on? You work harder than any of us. You eat less than we do. I don't understand it!'

George had been teaching the girls 'to talk proper', as John would say. John was as yet impervious to George's suggestions about correct English. 'I'm just talkin' the way my real dad talked. That's good enough fer me!'

Daughter Catherine continued, 'Come on, mum! No secrets in this house!'

Cathy sighed and smiled and finally gave in. 'Okay, okay, smarty-pants! Six months time, you might be having a little brother. I didn't want to tell you straight off because it might distract you from those real important projects, like the dam and the market garden. But now yer know! So just keep on working!' As a result of George's coaching, Cathy's use of colloquial English had diminished dramatically.

George said nothing. He simply smiled in an embarrassed fashion. John, the teenager who knew all about those things wanted to slap him on the back and say, 'Well done, George, old boy.' But he didn't. The other kids hadn't been able to work out why George had been so ecstatically happy over the last three months. He was uncharacteristically bubbly, cracking jokes and looking like the cat that had swallowed the cream. The truth was that he was somewhat embarrassed in the presence of his stepchildren about this baby-making business ... Suddenly, there were hugs all round!

Time for reflection! Cathy suddenly felt supremely powerful. Women have an amazing, miraculous capacity for generating human beings. Men might be the instigator, but women do the real work at perpetuating the human race. This capacity represents power and privilege. After the initial hesitation about when this should next happen, Cathy continued to thrive on her female role of contributing to an expanding world population. After her first child, Mary Anne, who didn't survive her first two weeks, Cathy hadn't missed a beat. She proceeded to double, triple, quadruple, quintuple, sestuple, septuple and now octuple her child-bearing capacity. What a miracle and what a privilege!

THE REAL FACTS OF LIFE

As you may know, if you have been researching books about procreation, during the first four weeks following conception, all embryos begin as females, endowed with female sex organs. So all of us, including the most of us virile tough guys, began our existence as females. It is only after week four that male characteristics begin to emerge. Who would have guessed? Certainly not the writers of the Adam and Eve story. The mythology of Eve's creation tells us that she was formed from Adam's rib. Modern science tells us a different story. Not that this is a problem for most of us 'true believers', knowing as we do that the Bible is based on myths and legends as well as history. The challenge is to sort out which is which.

George, now forty-one, was overjoyed. He had long feared that he might miss out on the thrill of parenthood. Decision-making and procrastination had been continuing challenges. He wanted to be sure about everything before making up his mind. Risk-taking was not part of his DNA. Procrastination most certainly was! But now that he had decided to take his courage in both hands, whether it be in choice of life partner or property purchase, he was overjoyed by the advantages of his new decisiveness. And now to top it off, he had demonstrated his capacity to generate children. He decided on the spot that there must surely be more where that came from. So he would set mind and body to the task in the ensuing years. This was to be the first of many!

Eliza Jane was born in January 1867 – not at home this time, but at the Amherst Hospital. George was most insistent. 'We might be dirt-poor. But my kid is going to be born in a real hospital as we do back home in Buckinghamshire. I want the best for any child of mine'.

The Amherst Hospital was eight miles away from Stoney Creek and three miles to the north-west of Talbot. Their little battered cart, drawn by the trusty Bullo, transported Cathy in style to the hospital. Despite the negative outcomes for many women in the hospitals of the middle 1800s, Amherst was regarded as a reputable hospital largely funded by gold. And, what's more, it was basically free of charge for those who couldn't afford it, which is why George always defined himself as a labourer rather than farmer when applying for hospital admission.

The reality was that in that era the survival rate for mothers-to-be who gave birth at home attended by an experienced midwife was double that of hospital births attended by a doctor. Cathy was fortunate to have hospital midwife Betty Johnson, who believed in washing her hands before delivering babies. Nurses and doctors had heard rumours about bacteria and clean hands. It wasn't until 1870 that it was recognised that these same bacteria caused septicaemia resulting in death for many mothers-to-be. It frequently happened that doctors attending to expectant mothers after handling corpses were one of the main causes of bacterial infection. Fortunately, Eliza Jane was brought into the world by the enlightened, hand-washing midwife, Betty Johnson.

Like the rest of the Kirby clan, new babe Eliza Jane was blessed with good health. Nevertheless, like most of the family, Eliza Jane Kirby would in the years to come be admitted to Amherst Hospital for various childhood afflictions. Her name is enshrined for all to see in the official Amherst Hospital records, where such conditions as persistent croup and a broken arm were recorded for posterity.

Serious illnesses in the Kirby/Lawson family were invariably attended to at the Amherst Hospital. This required an eight-mile drive by bullock cart to Amherst, which took about two hours. The bullocks Bullo and Bertrand had now experienced ten summers and ten winters in goldfield country. They were still in their prime. Between them, at the bidding of James, John and now George, they had loyally carted thousands of tons of lumber, rocks and soil. And now they were being asked to carry vegies to the market – embarrassing stuff!

George must have read their bovine minds and decided to look into the possibility of buying a horse. A good horse cost sixty pounds. He might get a hack for twenty. His good neighbour Cyril Soames had a crusty, ten-year-old nag which he no longer needed and which he was prepared to let go for a mere ten pounds. 'A bargain at twice the price!' declared George to Cathy as he snuggled against her bulging waistline.

So they invested in the ten-pound nag and called her Naggy. The main advantage of this acquisition was that horses travel faster than bullocks. The trip to the Clunes market now took one hour instead of two. And all for the irresistible price of ten pounds!

AN IRRESISTIBLE ASIDE

For some reason, we humans have a special affinity with the number ten. In fact we have made it the basis of our whole decimal system. We think of ten pounds as a nice, round, comfortable figure, echoed in recent times in the concept of the 'ten-pound Pom'. It may have started with that easy primitive counting system based on our ten fingers and ten toes. George the Pom would likewise have paid approximately ten pounds for his trip to Australia in the mid-eighteen hundreds. Ten continues to be a neat, satisfying figure, as in the Ten Commandments, the decimal system, school marks out of ten, the Ten Plagues, the logarithmic base ten, numbers from ten to one hundred to one thousand ad infinitum, the ten little nigger boys

*(which I insist should not be politically incorrect as it simply comes
from the Latin 'niger', meaning black).*

The naming ceremony for their newly purchased nag was simple. Cyril
had known him as Dobbin, a name that John felt was somewhat demean-
ing. It was time for rebirthing! What better name than Naggy! So Naggy
it became.

At ten years, Naggy was no longer her young and spritely self, but
she could still pull with ease the two-wheeled cart with the squeaky
wheels that went with the purchase. She could trot along at double the
pace of the oxen. They now had the luxury of two carts – the single shaft
ox cart and the double shaft horse-drawn version. Great for the thrice
weekly trips to the market, as well as emergency visits to the hospital!

Cathy breastfed Eliza Jane for six months instead of the usual
twelve. The new babe was a healthy seven-pounder and had an unlimited
appetite for mother's milk. The rest of the family, including four-year-old
Ellen, were kept busy working in the garden. When Eliza Jane reached
the six-month target, Cathy returned to work in the garden. Running back
and forth to the house every few hours to feed the baby was still a necessary chore. Young thirteen-year-old Catherine was happy to help out, as
she definitely preferred baby minding to digging up weeds. Eliza Jane
had begun to grow four healthy teeth and was starting to chew on chunks
of bread and meat. It was obviously a good time to stop breast-feeding!

Milk was still a significant part of Eliza Jane's diet. How did mothers in the 1860s continue to feed their newborns after, for whatever reason, they stopped breast-feeding? Glass babies' bottles had not yet been
invented. At first Cathy and young Catherine tried the used-cow-udder
system, with built-in teat. She acquired the udder at the Talbot meat
market. It worked quite well but proved to be unwieldy and somewhat
messy. Maybe there was a better way!

There was! George experimented with a cow horn. He cleaned out
the inside and ground out a tiny hole in the tip of the horn. He filled the

inside of the cow horn with milk, and controlled the flow with a finger on the hole or by tilting it so that the milk sat comfortably in the bend. Eliza Jane demonstrated her approval by quickly adapting to the new system of imbibing both mother's expressed milk and cow's milk. 'Well done.' said George to himself. 'Maybe I should patent it.'

It was now September. Spring was in the air. They were ahead of themselves. The Kirby/Lawson combination was working a treat. The dam was full to overflowing. The largest of the mineshafts, eight feet in diameter and twenty feet deep, was half full and ready for the bucket brigade. The other two mineshafts, which were about eight feet deep, were linked to the main mineshaft by two underground tunnels. They were both still empty. Nevertheless they had enough water to get started. They were now ready to embark on their market garden.

George had a brainwave – a windmill to pump the water to a header tank. This would give them a direct, effortless flow to the garden. A brilliant idea! Yes! But windmills cost money. George announced his plan to the family but reminded them, 'We mustn't put the cart before the horse. First we need to generate a bit of capital to be able to afford the luxury of a windmill.' They all knew about carts and horses so they caught on, right down to three-year-old Sarah. Gravity worked well for the dam, but when they had used up the dam water, for the time being it would be the bucket brigade from the mineshafts. The windmill was a dream that would materialise later.

Their market garden was ready for planting. The soil was moist, friable, free of stones and nourished by rotting vegetable matter and cow-manure. Their first crop would be potatoes, pumpkin, broad beans and cabbages.

'How about carrots!' shouted John. 'We all leeerve carrots!'

Cathy was the boss of the market garden.

'OK, John! And carrots!'

By the end of summer 1867, they had potatoes, pumpkin, broad beans, cabbages and carrots for sale. Out the front on a slab of ironbark attached to their post-and-rail fence they had a sign painted by George advertising their wares. He had added sketches of each vegetable, as many of the locals like George's own family were illiterate. John was fascinated by what appeared to him as indecipherable hieroglyphics. George had told John about the Egyptians and their word pictures called hieroglyphics. John's curiosity and will to learn new skills got the better of him, prompting him to ask George to share with him the mysteries of reading and writing. There was revolution in the air. On Sundays and rainy days, everyone except Cathy sat down with George and slowly learnt how to copy and decipher the twenty-six letters of the alphabet as well as such important words as mum, dad, cat, dog and potato.

They knew about the Kangaroo Gully School, a little wooden structure, which had appeared in 1865 a few miles away in the middle of the Stoney Creek forest. The school was soon to be known as the Stoney Creek state school. But Cathy was so fixated on growing vegetables that she insisted that they all work all day as a family on the garden.

'If we don't grow our vegies, we don't survive!' They all agreed they wanted to survive. No argument. There was no time for gallivanting off to school!

To survive those critical first twelve months, they had to beg and borrow. They balked at this second option because when you borrow you have to give back, which is difficult to do if you are living hand to mouth. As to that third un-named option, being essentially honest, they did not believe in it, except when it came to sneakily accessing water from their unnamed Stoney Creek tributary. Between themselves, every one except George called it Kirby Creek.

Luckily they had generous neighbours, particularly Cyril and Margery, who supported them in kind when they were desperate. A cabbage, a cauliflower, a bunch of carrots here and there helped stave off the hunger pangs. Payback time would come later when their first vegetables appeared.

In addition to the occasional loan or advance, doing odd jobs for aging neighbours and mutual assistance at harvest time kept the creditors at bay. They still had James' two bullocks, Bullo and Boris, which they continued to use to till the land and occasionally cart stuff for neighbours. They were more than beasts of burden. They were part of James' legacy. Despite their straitened circumstances, Cathy couldn't bring herself to part with them. Furthermore, bullocks, given their twenty-year lifespan, were in Cathy's mind worth their weight in gold, gold being the favoured currency in the Stoney Creek area. But the reality was that in the 1860s, Stoney Creek produced very few gold nuggets. The signs were there – specks of gold and occasional small undersized nuggets that teased hopeful prospectors. Shillings and pence and the occasional pound, in lieu of trading in real gold, were still very much in the mix.

Within six months, their market garden began to be productive. Their street art and vegie door sales attracted a handful of prospective customers, but the income generated was barely enough to cover costs. They needed to expand their marketing strategy. George and John stacked the old cart with potatoes, broad beans, pumpkins, cabbages and carrots and trundled off to Talbot market. In those days it opened from early morning till midday three times a week. There were plenty of hungry mouths looking for fresh and cheap vegetables. George was indeed their man!

Their farming enterprise was now a commercially viable business. Copper and occasional silver coins began rolling in. They tilled more land, expanded the farm to two acres, diversified to include winter vegetables like peas, beans, beetroot, cauliflower and spinach.

John, now twelve years old, made a few pence on the side helping with carting goods for successful miners and others in the nearby gold fields of Stoney Creek. The girls, including three-year-old Ellen, worked in the fields picking peas and beans, filling and carrying baskets and turning each little task into a game, a competition, with handicaps according to age, with a prize for the winner. It was fun as well as a means of surviving.

It was the middle of winter, 1868. The nights were cold, a good reason to snuggle up in bed to keep warm … and other things. George, for a second time, was to prove his virility. Suddenly Cathy was pregnant again. The score was currently six girls and one boy. Eliza Jane was now twelve months old, following the family tradition of knocking over her milk and throwing the occasional tantrum. That elusive second boy had to eventuate some time! Wasn't it all about crumbling cookies? No ultrasounds in those days! It was a game of wait-and-see. Cathy continued to work tirelessly on the farm, despite her bulging midriff.

Financially, it was still touch and go in so many ways. The budget was delicately balanced. Winter had come and gone. Spring was in the air. Their watering plan was working well. The arid soil had been regenerated. The crops were thriving. They now had brussels sprouts, tomatoes and pumpkin. Their giant Grosse Lisse tomatoes burst into life in the hot summer sun and were gobbled up voraciously by loyal customers at the Talbot market. The rains continued to fall – sporadically. The dam continued to perform its function – adequately. The coffers were mostly empty despite regular contributions. But at least they were no longer in debt. In fact, they were finally beginning to make ends meet. Bills were being paid on time! Gold-miners at nearby Talbot wanted vegetables. Talbot was expanding in all directions, and with it the population, and their family piggy bank – just like Cathy's waistline!

Cathy stopped working at eight months. Her dimensions were unusually generous. Suddenly the familiar pains began. George took Cathy off to Amherst Hospital, bouncing uncomfortably in the cart now drawn by Naggy.

The birth was more protracted and more challenging than in the past. But then it happened! More dramatically, more painfully, and finally more explosively than usual! And no wonder … It was a boy!. The nexus was broken. Cathy and George now had the longed-for boy – William Andrew.

Cathy was busy at home minding baby William and two-year-old Eliza Jane. During the day, the older girls continued to work in the vegetable garden with their usual energy. When they arrived home from the daily grind, it was all kisses and cuddles and gooing and gaaing for Little Willy, as he had now become. [It is interesting to note that in those days this name, as in current slang parlance, had specifically male biological connotations, coming from the Latin *membrum virile* meaning 'male member', *virile* becoming 'willy'.]

When George explained the impropriety of using such a name, John's response was, 'Who cares? I help change the nappies and I reckon it's spot on. He's a boy after all! Why pretend he's not!' So the new baby became simply, Little Willy.

John was quite possessive of his stepbrother, insisting that the 'step' appendage be discarded forthwith. John had six sisters and finally one brother. Because of the age difference, his new brother was not a rival as is often the case with siblings of similar age. John revelled in his role of protective big brother.

An Expanding Family

But there was one serious problem. The family was indeed expanding, but the house wasn't. The five girls were crammed into three double bunks, with room for just one more. John was still in the junk room with all the odds and sods. Cathy and George were in the room facing the garden with eighteen-month-old Eliza Jane in a crib that George had fashioned himself. Now they had to find room for another one of George's homemade cribs for Little Willy. The house desperately needed to expand. George now had great confidence in his baby-generating capacity. Cathy was still young enough to produce a few more!

'A farm needs many hands to make light work', George constantly reminded her.

'Yes, yes, Georgie darling!' responded Cathy. 'But we have to look to the *future*. Just like me, the house is bursting at the seams. This house needs to expand!'

Decisive action was needed. Cathy was the decision-maker. Someone needed to step up and put their hand to hammer and saw – now, not tomorrow or next week. Who other than George and John, this job being boys' stuff?

'OK, dear George and son, hop to it!' Being instinctively the consummate male psychologist, she added, 'I have the greatest confidence in you!'

On a sudden, George and John discovered within themselves a new and unsuspected talent – that of housebuilding. John was sixteen, could now read and write in a rudimentary way, had opinions on everything, and had started to challenge parental authority. They sat down together to discuss their options, and like many incipient house-builders, quite appropriately, they formed a *board* of three people – Cathy, George and John. After serious discussion and a certain amount of obfuscation, they decided to add two more rooms for sleeping and whatever, and a front veranda, and a lean-to at the back for a laundry, and an odds and sods room, just like James' original log cabin.

George and John were to spread the work over six months. Their primary task was running the farm. But at the same time, they were required by Cathy to create time for the building project. Both George and John had to admit that they felt good about themselves, flexing their muscles, thinking out problems, and seeing the project grow before them. Their dream was to finish the job before another probable new baby arrived. John was slightly pessimistic about their prospects, summing up with:

'Not bloody likely! But we'll give it a good go!' So in the meantime, they took it for granted that they'd have two bubs with them in the master bedroom.

'Let's hope this one's not a screamer!' muttered George to himself, forgetting for the moment that is was all his fault.

They dug stump holes for ironbark posts, laid bearers and joists of stringy bark, and constructed walls with braces, applying Pythagoras's views on right-angled triangles. George remembered all about Pythagoras from his English Grade 8 education. On top of each wall was a wall plate that supported ceiling joists and rafters and which in turn supported their pitched roof. The outside of the original house was covered in split stringybark palings. They followed the same method for their extension. Making split-paling doors was quite easy. They made a frame with halving joints on the corners and nailed on overlapping split palings. So simple!

Hinges were an interesting challenge. The traditional farmhouse system was cutting up old shoes, salvaging the leather, and nailing two by four inch strips to door and frame. Unfortunately they had no spare shoes. Steel hinges had to be made by a blacksmith and were quite pricey.

'I know!' said John. 'How about we try the Talbot junk market!'

George's response: 'Great idea, Johnny my boy! Let's do just that! You're not just a pr … handsome face!'

John was the first to see it – a stack of rusty ancient hinges of irregular shapes. Perfect!

'We clean 'em up with a bit 'er animal fat, scrub 'em with a handful of dirt to get the rust off and Bob's your uncle.'

George couldn't let it go. 'Or as the French would say – *voilà*!' He was into affirming seventeen-year-old John every chance he had. A good relationship was so important to George, given that his connection with his own father at the same age was rather average.

The windows were the tricky bit. They had bought some second-hand window glass from a mate. They were going to make the extension fit the window frames, and the frames fit the second-hand panes of glass. From the Amherst timber mill, they acquired some milled four by one and a half hardwood. They joined the sides using halving joints, which they glued and nailed. Then came the delicate task of chiselling a groove for the glass. Gently does it – one splinter at a time, watching the direction of the grain, and carefully shaping the channel for the glass! George, assuming he was in charge, reminded seventeen-year-old John rather portentously:

'If you hit the chisel too hard, my boy, and don't watch the grain, you can lose the whole bloody lot in one go.' And he added, asserting his parental authority, 'So go easy! We're almost finished, Johnny-boy. Don't muck it up!'

John's cheeky response was, 'Whatever you say, Stepdad! You're der boss. I'm der lackey. I must admit yer doin' a fair enough job fer an old feller!' They were such great mates, really!

Eight months later, the ironbark veranda posts were in place and reasonably vertical, and the roofing joists and battens were firmly fixed at eighteen-inch centres. They had finished the framework for the low-pitched front veranda, at the same time extending the length of the house. At the back they had completed the skeleton for the lean-to laundry and odds and sods room. All was ready for the split-paling cladding and the wrought-iron roofing.

For the roof, they managed to squirrel up the wherewithal to purchase a stash of second-hand roofing iron that was still in good condition.

'It's the sea air that does the damage. But this stuff lasts well out here in the sticks,' said George.

'You're right again, Stepdad!'

Corrugated wrought iron roofing was coming down in price. There was a lot of it on the second-hand market after the fires, in various degrees of good condition. Their building program was on track.

It was time to talk about the 'Stepdad' appellation. George was sick of it.

'John, I mean Johnny, we're such good mates, aren't we?'

'Yer, sure! Whatever yer say, Stepdad.'

'Well, I reckon it's time you called me *Dad* or *George*. I don't like *Stepdad*!'

John responded affirmatively.

'OK Stepd … I mean, *Georgie!*'

George butted in.

'I prefer *George,* not *Georgie,* if you don't mind. It's more respectful and dignified.'

John lost it. His reply was simple and direct.

'Bugger respectful and dignified! It's *Georgie* or back to *Stepdad*. Take yer pick!'

Through gritted teeth, George responded:

'OK! You win. For the sake of peace, *Georgie* it is!'

'Rightio, if you absolutely insist, Georgie! But from now on I'd really prefer to call you *George*!'

Teenagers of all eras love taking the Mickey out of their elders. Seventeen-year-old John was no exception.

The dunny would remain on its noisome ownsome in the middle of the backyard, a prey to blowflies, wasps and redbacks. The first thing you would do was check for whatever biting creature might be lurking there ready to attack vulnerable parts of the human anatomy. At night, most of the family had formed the habit of approaching this gloomy, rickety structure armed with hurricane lantern and an appropriate weapon. Once inside, if you're on a sit-down mission, having checked for marauders, you'd balance on a fixed four-inch bough athwart an evil-smelling, six-foot hole in the ground. If you slipped, the consequences were quite disastrous. John took great pleasure in stretching out this word to *diz-arse-ter-rers* to the horror and delight of his sisters. They regularly purchased newspapers – for the news, yes, or for perusing the pictures and the ads, but more importantly for tearing up into six-inch squares and skewering on a nail on the dunny wall.

The only change to the amenities was carving out a serviceable toilet seat. George souvenired a wide slab of stringy bark and cut it to shape with his trusty old bow saw. He carefully scraped off most of the splintery bits and attached his newly carved masterpiece with strips of old boot leather to the horizontal back beam. What a luxury, especially appreciated by the girls! It worked well apart from the occasional splinter for that particularly vulnerable part of the human anatomy. At least the chance of slipping into the noisome depths was significantly minimised.

All of these home improvements were achieved well in advance of the rapid succession of newborns over the next seven years – the inevitable result of early weaning. Babies were to keep coming at about eighteen-month intervals till Cathy reached menopause. The George and Cathy team boasted of six offspring during their time together. Cathy's children numbered thirteen in total, counting Mary Jane who you will remember died shortly after birth.

The junk from John's bedroom was spread around to various cupboards and corners of the newly renovated house. After six months Willy was weaned, with good reason. His baby teeth were starting to break through. Also Cathy wanted to continue her organising role in the vegie patch. They took turns at baby-minding and more recently baby-feeding. As they did for Eliza Jane, there was George's amazing invention of the cow-horn system. The advantage was that it was light and easy to clean, and the flow of milk to the baby was easily controlled by tilting at the appropriate angle. Ah! The marvels of goldfields technology!

John made a sterling contribution to jobs requiring physical strength. George ran the farm, did the marketing, and between times worked like a Trojan with his good mate John on the innumerable physical tasks that confront a farmer. As the farm grew in size, they would certainly need a new injection of male muscle for such jobs as ploughing, tree felling and fencing. William Andrew was the answer to their prayers. All they had to do was be patient. They tell us that time flies. It was possible that John, now seventeen, would not be there on the farm forever unless his status and birth right were specifically defined *en famille*! The eldest would normally inherit the property, but was John really interested in a lifetime of farming? These were serious matters to be pondered.

Meantime, they continued to rejoice in the presence within the family of Little Willy. Boy babies were all too often spoilt rotten and overfed. Because of the incessant daily snacks, Little Willy was becoming quite a whopper. They changed his name to 'Whopper Willy'. He must have understood because suddenly he began to lose his baby fat as he toddled around the house and garden. He now became simply 'Willy'.

To further celebrate this new promise of prosperity, at Cathy's urging and with an eye to the future, George set off for the Clunes market, his mission being to invest in five two-week-old calves, thereby adding dairy products and meat to their market potential. Once again mateship helped him bolster his depleted finances. He had four pounds in the piggy bank. Newborn calves went for two pound a pop. George decided to bend his rules on borrowing. By using the 'save, beg and borrow' combination, he was able to make his dream a reality. That evening George and John arrived home with four girl calves and one boy calf, the beginning of their planned herd.

They tethered these delightful but voracious baby bovines in various grass-rich spots around the farm. Fortunately calves could be weaned at two weeks. At that stage, they began to munch away contentedly at the variegated local herbage with their baby teeth. They topped off their repast by ruminating as bovines do, reprocessing the grass and chewing their cud. As a matter of urgency, George and John set about putting up more fences around the property, creating three different areas to enable the grass to regenerate scientifically.

George and John had established a real sense of mateship, despite early resistance. George had finally convinced John about the advantages of learning to read and write. John no longer espoused the view: 'What's good enough for Mum is good enough for me.' So stepson, aided and abetted by stepfather, were now making real progress in the formidable task of conquering the alphabet, and then making sense of those disparate symbols juxtaposed in a particular way as to convey meaning.

Cathy looked over their shoulders on occasion, and step-by-step she discovered that literacy was not such a scary proposition. Nevertheless, she remained an onlooker, never wanting to get involved in this book-learning business. Books and newspapers were now becoming part of the furniture.

The Kirby/Lawson farm was to be a three-acre vegetable produce farm, with a further twenty acres of grazing land that would comfortably accommodate the needs of up to fifteen cattle. There was about an acre of stringybark messmate in the bottom corner, which they used for firewood and construction jobs. In one year's time, two of their calves would provide an important source of revenue at the meat market. Possessing the facility to reproduce themselves, these accommodating bovines ensured an appropriate balance between calves and adult cattle. Apart from providing meat and milk, their job was to keep down the grass on the twenty acres of pasture, thus minimising the risk of grass-fires. So the Kirby/Lawson farm was defined by vegetables and cattle. But the backbone of this farming venture was the continuous source of revenue generated by the reliable workforce of women needed for the labour-intensive vegetable growing.

George, for the umpteenth time, shared his thoughts with Cathy. 'We need more young farmhands, as the older ones will soon be looking for pastures new. Sooner or later, some of our kids will leave the nest to get married. So let's get cracking, my beautiful, darling Catherine!' The new George calculated details about crops, acreage, popular vegetables, current prices, Chinese competition, rainfall, water sources, drought, bush-fire-proofing, and last but not least – expanding the family. He constantly wrote notes and plans and drew up graphs. His conclusion was quite simply expressed in the oft-repeated dictum: 'The more the merrier!'

George was no longer the classic procrastinator.

Martha Deborah was to eventuate nine months later. George shrugged his shoulders and agreed that girls were OK too. After all, they performed as well as any boy in the vegie garden. Cathy insisted they were even better because they didn't slack off and didn't constantly look for excuses like chopping trees and didn't boast about their special boy expertise in driving Naggy to the vegie market.

Then disaster struck! It was in the summer of 1871. The forest was dry as tinder. In preparation for the dry spell, George had made sure that the grass was kept at bay on the Kirby/Lawson property. The most important part of his fire plan was the voracious appetites of the cattle. Fortunately, this time the fires did not reach Stoney Creek.

The town of Amherst eight miles to the north and its surroundings were severely impacted by a devastating, all-consuming bushfire. George and John and many of the locals set off for Amherst to help fight the fires. They were driven by self-interest as much as community spirit. They knew that bushfires could travel like the wind. Many of the properties around Amherst fell victim to the unforgiving flames. Fortunately the hospital survived. Eighteen houses were burnt to the ground. The fires were ultimately contained without loss of life.

The forest at Stoney Creek continued to be supremely vulnerable. A fire driven by the north wind could reach them in no time. On the positive side, the influx of wannabe miners meant that much of the forest had been cut back, and there was a significant workforce to fight the fires if necessary. But there was no such thing as the Country Fire Brigade. This community-based, fire-fighting service didn't eventuate until the end of the century. Meanwhile, their best hope was the firebreak, or a wind change, or rain, or at worst thrashing the fire into submission with wet bags and green tree branches. They remained prepared for the worst. This time luck was on their side.

Farming and genealogy will continue to dominate our story. On the one hand, we have the burgeoning farm – a farm that depended on a workforce of eight, made up of parents and growing children. On the other, we have the procreative energies of the two main players, Cathy and George. Because Cathy has now begun to wean her offspring earlier, the contraceptive effect of extended breastfeeding meant that childbirth could occur sooner rather than later and with increasing regularity. The one hundred pound question was how many children would be generated before menopause kicked in.

Both George and Cathy worked on the principle that the more children the more cheap, easily accessed labour at their disposal, and that ultimately that elusive dream called 'prosperity' would become a reality. They also espoused the view that big families were close families, which in practice was very much the case given the limited available space. Furthermore, George believed in educating his children. He was an ardent advocate for skills in reading, writing and arithmetic. Just as he himself had had a good primary school education to Grade 8 in Buckinghamshire, he wanted the same for his children.

The Clunes primary school was too far away and difficult to access, while the new Stoney Creek school was in its infancy and yet unproven. Neither Cathy nor her first six children were interested in schooling. The farm came first. George believed that nibbling away at these skills at night, on Sundays and on rainy days would provide the family with these essential life skills. He had already imparted rudimentary reading skills to John. He would progressively work on the whole family.

An important start for Cathy and John had been learning how to sign their names with meaningful letters rather than with the lazy 'X'. Cathy now knew how to sign her name, but she stubbornly refused to do so, just as her own mum Mary had, declaring: 'What's good enough for my ma is good enough for me!'

Because of Cathy's mindset, it was too late and impractical to send any of her first six children to school. They all preferred to be a part of the Kirby work force rather than waste time on book-learning.

Such was not the case with Cathy and George's six children. Several years previously, in 1864, the Stoney Creek residents had cleared a small patch of land and built themselves a wooden school, twenty-four by fourteen feet, at the cost of thirty-five pounds. The new brick school, built in 1869 at a cost of two hundred and forty-three pounds, was a much better proposition. James Knight was the highly respected principal. The first Kirby/Lawson child to attend the school was five-year-old Eliza Jane in 1873. All of the subsequent children were to attend the school, obviously at the insistence of George. It meant a two-mile trudge via road and bush from home to school. The school was at its height in 1876 when the real Stoney Creek gold rush eventuated. Eliza Jane, William and Martha were at school during this period. Business was brisk. Optimistic miners with the gleam of gold in their eyes flocked to Stoney Creek.

'The more the merrier!' declared Cathy.

'Just keep churning out those vegies!' declared George.

Amherst Hospital records tell us that over the next six years, George and Cathy generated three more children – one more boy and two more girls. It seems that menopause kicked in when Cathy was forty-four.

Below is a list of George and Cathy's children and their year-of-birth records, of which five out of six took place at Amherst Hospital, eight miles away from their home at Stoney Creek.

1867 June ELIZA JANE Amherst Hospital
1869 March WILLIAM ANDREW Amherst Hospital
1870 December MARTHA Amherst Hospital
1872 July BENJAMIN Amherst Hospital
1874 May MARY Amherst Hospital
1876 March SARAH Stoney Creek (home birth)

Six children over ten years. It appears that early weaning was prompted by the needs of adult supervision in their burgeoning market garden. Growing, harvesting and selling were all-consuming jobs. Cathy wanted to get back on the job as soon as possible after the birth of each child. Hence the approximate eighteen-month gap between children.

Meanwhile, George was totally engaged in selling produce at the Stoney Creek and Talbot markets, as well as building fences and attending to the cattle. The market garden continued to be Cathy's sole responsibility. Competition from Chinese market gardeners had not yet seriously impacted on the local fruit and veg market to the same extent as in the Clunes area. Stoney Creek had its own challenges. Sustainable crops with limited water resources continued to need hard work and intelligent organisation. Under Cathy's watchful eye and given her focused organising ability, the crops not only survived but thrived, according to the seasons and market demands. Cathy and her team worked tirelessly. In the interests of the vegie garden, she breast-fed for six months and then it was back to the grind. From that point on, it was cow's milk for baby Martha, then Ben, and ultimately for Mary and Sarah. No wonder there were such short gaps between children!

But it worked both ways. On the one hand, the older girls had to attend to the babies of the house, depriving the garden of a part of its much-needed workforce. On the other hand, the original six (James' children) were growing older, more experienced and more productive, which put them slightly ahead in the market versus the child-rearing game. It would all come out in the wash.

There were three boys to ten girls. John was sixteen years older than his little brother William, and nineteen years older than Benjamin. George knew his Bible well. The biblical youngest of Jacob's twelve male offspring was named Benjamin. Evidently George guessed that this would be his last boy-child, boys being hard to come by. God certainly works in mysterious ways, considering that Cathy's ultimate tally was ten girls and three boys. The last two were girls – Mary and Sarah. The last three had popular, biblical names but no second name. Maybe George and Cathy thought that thinking up second names was unnecessary and too much like hard work. Why bother if the first name is the only one used in day-to-day communication? And maybe, given their marital status, they wanted to make peace with God by giving unadorned biblical names to the last four – Martha, Benjamin, Mary, Sarah.

We now go back in time to 1873, the year of the Chinese riots at nearby Clunes. All was blissfully calm at Talbot and Stoney Creek. Benjamin had graced the scene in July of the previous year. There was a distinctive kind of familial love in the air. But ten miles away at nearby Clunes a festering unrest was brewing. Up till the advent of the Chinese, all had been relatively calm. There was the occasional murder, a death from a collapsing mineshaft, minor skirmishes about who staked what claim and when. But there was no serious civil unrest – until the Chinese moved in. They were inveterate workers and the first sign of trouble was when they began to strike it rich. The problem was that 'these pig-tailed heathen' were prepared to work in the mines seven days a week. The miners of European extraction insisted on taking a traditional half-day off on Saturday, and, for most, a day for rest or worship on Sunday. They were unhappy about these hard-working heathens, and they were ready to rumble.

Buses of Chinese miners, accompanied by police, arrived at Clunes to claim their rights. The accompanying police and the busloads of Chinese were assailed by angry miners and their wives, armed with pick-axes and waddies. They attacked the buses with a hail of rocks, smashing windows and yelling insults at these despised Orientals. The Chinese interlopers were driven out of Clunes. Many headed for such places as Talbot where they joined a more tolerant multicultural workforce. There they diversified. As well as continuing to mine, many turned their attention to market-gardening.

Predictably, the result was lower market prices. Potatoes were the Kirby staple product. They produced them cheaply and in abundance. Fortunately they had established a loyal customer base that had faith in Cathy's famous Irish spuds. Spinach, swedes, turnips, carrots, celery and silver beet were still very much in the mix, and produced efficiently and in abundance by the Kirby family-based, unpaid child-labour enterprise. It wasn't easy, but with hard work and careful organisation, they were able to compete with the Chinese whose fruit and vegies were the product of a workforce made up of single, hard-working males. The 'Chinks' as the miners called them, were far away from their homeland, and focused on sending money back to China to support their families. As for the Kirby/Lawson conglomerate, they survived the market pressures by adding cattle to the mix. It was a ploy that helped them to survive market pressures and balance their precarious budget.

In the spring of 1873, four new calves were born – two males and two females. To increase the herd, they headed off to the Talbot market where they invested in another four two-week-old male calves, which they proceeded to turn into steers. The other two male calves were to suffer the same fate. George and John performed the operation. Both were thoroughly squeamish at the prospect. The girls stayed inside. With this weird feeling that their own masculinity was being threatened, the men tied the first calf's legs together and proceeded to excise the unwanted appendages. John's bottom lip quivered and George had a tear in his eye. John held the frightened calf down and George wielded the knife. The calf wailed in fear and pain. They released the ropes and off it scampered. Twenty minutes later they had six steers, six cows and one bull, making up their total of thirteen bovines.

Two of the cows were sent to the meat market. For the moment the bull had a reprieve. He still had work to do. They had to balance milk and beef production. Their relatively small property could handle a maximum of fifteen cattle, depending on drought conditions and the possibility of bushfires, which were a constant threat. George's early dream of twenty cattle was too optimistic given the dry conditions in the goldfields.

The wildfire that occurred just before the Christmas of 1873 almost destroyed them. It started from a campfire in the miners' camp at Kangaroo Gully, which was the old name for Stoney Creek. This time, these north-wind-driven fires spared Amherst and Talbot and focused their attention on the Stoney Creek Forest and surrounding properties. The Kirby/Lawson family drove the cattle to the dam. Their bucket brigade and their new hand-operated pump saved them from the flames that roared through their property and threatened to engulf them.

The trees at the low end were the first to go. Then the flames roared through the grass like a steam train despite the good work done by the cattle. They stood waiting with their buckets and green tree branches ready to thrash the flames into submission. One minute later they were engulfed in billowing smoke. They coughed and struggled for breath. With smarting eyes, they threw buckets of water hither and thither and beat at the flames with their boughs. They stood bravely around their market garden extinguishing spot fires that converged on their beloved vegies. Finally the stifling heat forced them to run for their lives. But they had made a difference. The vegies were singed but not destroyed. As they retreated backwards towards the house, the wind began to change direction as a welcome southerly came to bear. Gradually they had the flames under control. They stamped down the glowing embers, finishing off with a few well-directed buckets of water from the well.

'We've won!' shouted Lizzy.

Annie responded with: 'If hell's like that, I'm gunna be good from now on!'

They were lucky. Fortunately the cattle had kept most of the grass down, and they had a well-prepared fire plan. But a wildfire is difficult to contain, particularly if driven by a fierce north wind. The dam and the mineshaft water reserves proved a Godsend. Cathy, the eternal optimist, rounded off with her favourite saying:

'All's well that ends well!'

George winced at John's summation. 'Yer! We done real good!'

'Well done, team! The house, the cattle and *us* have all survived.'

Even George occasionally got his grammar wrong! Some of their vegetables had succumbed, given the ferocity of the heat. Their pasture had been devastated by the flames. At the lower end of the property, the forest of stringybarks stood starkly black totally denuded of leaves.

'Have no fear! They'll bounce back!' declared George portentously. He added with the authority of a typical eighteenth century pedagogue: 'Stringybarks have got this layer of thick furry bark that protects them from fires – provided the fires don't burn too hot.'

Ever the teacher, he added: 'A wind-driven fire comes and goes so fast that most of your trees survive. They lose their leaves, but in time they are back as good as ever.' George had spoken! They knew that he was right as usual.

'You bewdy!' said John. 'George, you're a genius! What you don't know about burnt trees is not worth knowing!' They all gave a communal sigh of relief.

George hadn't finished yet. 'Yes! In two years' time, they will be as good as new with brand new leaves, but their trunks will remain black forever!'

'Aw, bloody hell!' said John. 'I'm gunna miss that bewdiful brown stringy look!'

Their neighbours, Cyril and Margaret Considine and Harry and Beth Osborne had lost their houses as well as their crops. The township of Stoney Creek itself fared worse than most of the farms. But it could have been worse. The fire had passed as quickly as it arrived. George and his family turned their attention to helping out neighbours. The toll included not only the two neighbouring farmhouses but also thirteen homes from within the struggling mining town of Stoney Creek, a prey to a merciless north-wind-driven fire that took no prisoners.

The bull had indeed survived the fire. But he didn't realise that he was soon destined for the meat market, and a different kind of heat that would turn him into roast beef. They didn't need a bull. It was so much easier to replenish the herd with two-week-old calves at two quid a pop at the Talbot Farmers' Market. Food for thought: meat on their plates, and money in their pockets!

Finding fodder for the cattle wasn't easy. The price of feed went up overnight. They were helped by the generosity of farmers in the neighbouring valley. These neighbours were fortunate enough to have low-lying fields that survived the devouring flames. There was still enough fodder to go round. George and Cathy's denuded fields were a minor blip that sorted itself out as the pastures regenerated. Three months later, autumn rains began to fall and the bare paddocks were soon on the road to recovery. In fact, the fire gave them a new lease of life. The grass was greener, the blackened eucalypts sprouted new leaves, the vegies revived, the cows mooed happily, the bull proclaimed his male dominance with an occasional bellow when not munching contentedly at the verdant new grass. George was right!

Their bull indeed didn't know that his days were numbered. In the following spring, successful miners would have juicy steaks on their plates, steaks that sold at the market at twenty pence a pound. A one-ton bull, after costs of butchering and the time and effort required to sell the meat at the market, meant thirty extra pounds in George's pocket. They didn't need an under-utilised bull. It was time to capitalise on their investment.

It was also time to implement George's windmill plan. When Harry Osborne lost his house to the fires, he also lost his windmill. The tank and blades had survived despite a few dents and bends, but the timber stand had not. What was left lay amongst the weeds where the windmill had once proudly stood. Harry and Beth Osborne had had enough.

'We're both too old for this caper. We're gunna sell up and move to Clunes and look after the grandkids while son Jack works at the mines. Mabel'll do a bit of house-cleaning on the side and we'll both mind the kids.'

George's mind was turning over. 'What are you going to do with what's left of the windmill?'

'Flog it off, of course, unless you're interested.'

'Maybe! I just sold my bull. How would thirty pounds in your pocket sound?'

'Bloody great! Let's shake on it! It's a deal!' George smiled his secret, satisfied smile.

'I hope yer made the right decision, father George' said John. 'The blades are bent, there's a dent in the tank and the whole lot's black and rusty!'

George responded with his usual optimism, slipping into John's lingo, 'She'll be jake, mate! So keep your shirt on! Between us, we can patch it up! Easy-peasy!'

Johnny roared with laughter and slapped his stepdad on the back and responded with:

'By jolly old gad, Faarrther. Absolutely topping! We'll make an Aussie out of you yet!'

If he had lived in the era of 'My Fair Lady', he might have added, 'By George, you've got it!'

Cathy's response was, 'Well done boys! I'm proud of you! I love yer both, and my vegies'll love yer too!'

George and John lugged the remains of Harry's old windmill and tank, complete with pump, over to the cart and loaded it all on. Then they set off for the old mine site.

'OK, Johnny, me boy, let's get cracking! You scrub it up and I'll handle the dents, and we'll build the stand together. We'll use those logs we stashed under the house.'

By the end of the week, the stand was completed, the tank was in place beside their deepest mine shaft. It was high enough to provide gravity-fed water to the vegie garden. They waited for the wind till early afternoon. Suddenly, the vanes began to turn, the pump began to pump, and the water began to flow – slowly, inexorably, drop by dribble, into the tank. The dribble became a steady pulsating flow. Two days later the tank was full.

'Aren't we clever, George old man!'

'Yes, Johnny, you cheeky young fellow! Aren't *I*!'

They could now run water from the dam and the overhead tank to the garden using the force of gravity and without the need of man-power, woman-power or girl-power. Their energies could be directed to cultivating, growing, herding, milking, selling and, of course, surviving.

Cathy and George were as stubborn as ever about their Catholic as against Church of England marital status. Their religious differences continued to simmer within the depths of their respective psyches. Whenever there was reference to God or a Bible story, it was never in the context of a particular religion. The closest they got to an agreement was when they were at risk of losing all to the bushfires. They had prayed together for God to protect them from the ravages of the firestorm, which God did. Nevertheless, Cathy continued to stubbornly proclaim her non-church-going Catholicism, and George, the dyed-in-the-wool Protestant, clung to his Anglican mind-set. It seemed that never the twain were destined to meet.

They were still unmarried in the eyes of each church. The children continued to take Cathy's married name. They were all Kirbys. There-fore George Lawson's children were: Eliza Jane Kirby, William Andrew Kirby, Martha Kirby, Benjamin Kirby, Mary Kirby and Sarah Kirby. It rankled, for sure, but not enough to cause a major showdown. George was prepared to bide his time. But for the moment he had to admit defeat in not passing on the Lawson name to his offspring. He told himself and them that he loved them as much whatever their surname. As the edu-cated Protestant Pommy who had studied Shakespeare at his old Buckinghamshire school, he would spout forth his favourite Shakespearean mantra from *Romeo and Juliet*:

> *'What's in a name? That which we call a rose*
> *By any other name would smell as sweet.'*

But, deep down, he didn't believe it. They were both equally stubborn. In her own way, Cathy knew she was the victor. Her Catholic identity defined her. It was part of her Irishness. As much as she would have loved a proper wedding ceremony, it would not be at the cost of her essential Catholicity. All of her children, including George's six, remained for the most part deep-rooted Kirbys.

There were two exceptions to the rule – school enrolments and hospital admissions. Whenever they were admitted to the Amherst Hospital, parents' names and occupation had to be provided. George, who signed all the documents, identified himself as the husband and parent.

For the books, his occupation was labourer instead of farmer so as to access the no-charge option available to the working poor. Therefore, for hospital admissions they all signed in as Lawsons including Cathy. As parent and prime signatory, it was George's practice to sign his name as 'George Lawson' in firm, clear handwriting.

During the Kirby/Lawson era, the family accessed hospital services quite frequently. George's signature in 1866 was clear and neatly formed. By 1870, when George was forty-five, it had become shaky and awkward. By 1876 he chose to use the X like Cathy as his health mysteriously began to deteriorate. Whether it was because these services were available at no cost or because as time went by they were afflicted by more serious health problems, hardly a year went by without someone being in hospital.

According to Amherst Hospital records, Margaret Kirby, on 11 August 1871, now being fourteen years of age, was admitted suffering a mysterious debilitating illness. Margaret was Cathy and James' third surviving child, the gentle, conscientious one. To save the water in the house overhead water tank, she had been accessing water from the mineshafts, which were all quite full in the winter of 1871. The mineshaft water was kept primarily for the garden. Catherine, the thoughtful, caring one, had been using this water for bathing and drinking. She did not see the dead possum floating within the dark confines of that mineshaft, nor was she aware of whatever contamination might be lurking there from the mining era. What did the miners dump into those shafts? Was the lead used in separating gold from dross a part of the problem?

Whatever the explanation, something in the mineshafts that did not affect the water used for the market gardens may have been a source of contamination destined to attack Margaret's delicate constitution. Margaret became afflicted by the dreaded illness of septicaemia. Cathy was both mystified and devastated.

'George, do something! This is serious.' George, who believed in doctors and hospitals, indeed did something. Catherine was whisked off to the Amherst Hospital in their horse-drawn cart where she was attended to by the well meaning, pseudo-doctor, Mr J. Adams.

Mr Adams was the product of the old barber-surgeon system. He was not a qualified doctor, but he was an experienced orderly. Diagnosis was not his long suit. Many diseases had similar symptoms. He knew vaguely about such deadly diseases as tuberculosis, smallpox, cholera, typhus and diphtheria. His solution for all things was a long stay in hospital and treatment with a range of popular panaceas. These included sundry elixirs and syrups, and, of course, milk of magnesia and, at worst, laudanum. This was an era when doctors did not understand the nature or cause of infection. Pasteur identified the existence of germs in the 1860s. His theories were not broadly accepted till the 1880s. The Kirby/Lawson family, like everyone else, were a prey to all kinds of potentially deadly diseases that were passed on by contamination. The accepted solution was a long term in hospital, when with any luck the immune system would kick in. The good news is that bodies tend to cure themselves. Or is it God who does it when he created humanity with the capacity to recover in time from most illnesses? The family certainly prayed together for Margaret's cure.

Fifty-five days later, Mr J. Adams declared Margaret cured. Meanwhile the dead possum had been removed from the mineshaft and the water had been diluted by constant use. The Kirby/Lawson family had not established the connection between the dead possum and Margaret's illness. They were just as mystified when she developed the same symptoms five years later. Maybe this time it was the dead mice floating in the main house water tank. These little critters had apparently run along the gutter, dislodged the wire mesh and slipped down the inflow pipe into the water-tank. The rest of the family had apparently developed immunity against water-born contamination, but not Margaret, given her delicate constitution. Their solution was once again Amherst Hospital and the worthy Mr Adams, who they believed had successfully cured her last time.

Subsequently, hospital documentation, which had been rescued from the fires that destroyed the building in 1914, triumphantly declared once again:

*MARGARET KIRBY – 18 years old, daughter of James and
Catherine Laughlin, left the hospital 1/7/1876 after 46 days ...
CURED.*

A Dastardly Melodrama

atherine, Cathy's first surviving daughter was not so lucky. It was 1878. Catherine was twenty-five years of age. She longed for her independence and dearly wanted to have a man in her life. She worked as a domestic at the home of Mr and Mrs Arblaster of Talbot to supplement the Kirby/Lawson tight household budget. She managed to put aside a little spending money for herself but most of her earnings went to the family. Chinese competition in the sale of vegetables was stiff, so every little bit counted.

Every day of the week except Sunday, Elizabeth, Annie and Ellen continued to work with their mother in the market garden. Catherine, the independent twenty-five-year-old, had to make her own way to Clunes every morning. This meant a five-mile walk each way, except when she managed to hitch a ride with a passing horse-drawn vehicle. Those were the days when you trusted people, and when offering a ride to those on foot was not viewed with suspicion. It was simply what you did – a kindness offered and accepted.

Catherine was the happy-go-lucky one, who trusted everyone. She spent the day minding children, wiping bottoms, washing dishes and scrubbing floors. But there was someone else in the house that was interested in her for more than her housekeeping skills. It was twenty-six-year-old Arthur, 'call-me-Arty', Arblaster. Arthur suffered an aversion for any kind of work, and his parents tolerated his laziness. Arthur spent his days mooching around the house doing nothing, until he became aware of this charming addition to the household. He fixed his predatory eye on Catherine. With practised patter, he soon won her over with his engaging smile and bubbly small talk. Catherine, expert at recognising Irish blarney, did not immediately recognise the English type.

Two days later, Arthur accosted her again as she was hanging nappies on the line. He approached casually enough. But suddenly with disconcerting earnestness he assumed the role of the insistent lover.

'Catherine, my dear, I can no longer pretend!' Catherine was flattered by his attentions but also embarrassed.

He went on: 'The first time I saw you, I fell for your bewitching brown eyes and your cute Irish freckles.'

All Catherine could respond was, 'Really?'

As the days went on, he repeatedly assured her that it must be love at first sight, although she was undoubtedly 'below his station'. The only 'station' Catherine knew was the railway one in the middle of Talbot. But she fell for it. Talk about wish-fulfilment blandishments! Soon he was whispering in her receptive ear about a possible 'blissful future'. Catherine, despite her familiarity with blarney, finally succumbed, induced by the promises of this scheming philanderer.

Two weeks later, Mother was out with her social set, and the brats were off at school. Before Catherine knew it, she was lying on a couch in fond embrace with this enticing young shyster. Too late! He dragged at her clothing. He was stronger than he looked. Catherine fought back. But he was too strong for her. The inevitable happened. She screamed and scratched. She went down fighting.

Conscience-stricken, Catherine dragged back on her dishevelled clothing and ran for the door, sobbing with embarrassment and totally guilt-ridden. As we know, it is a sad fact of life that all too often young women in this situation take on the guilt and blame themselves. She just kept running the whole five miles home.

Catherine the daughter fell into the arms of Catherine the mother and shared with her the whole sordid story. Cathy upbraided her roundly.

'How could you fall for the oldest trick in the book?'

'I'm so sorry, Mum!'

'How many times have I warned you? Wait till your father comes home!'

'I'm sorry, I'm sorry, I'm sorry! I just didn't know! He sounded so nice, at first!'

'You better hide in the back room while I try to settle him down. It takes a lot to get him riled, but I'm telling you now, he'll kill the bastard and probably you with him!'

Cathy and family had never seen George in such a rage. He was usually the self-contained, gentle father figure. But not this time! He roared and blasphemed in an uncharacteristic manner and called his daughter a 'mindless slut'. The other children cowered behind the door. John, for the first time in his life, was lost for words.

Catherine crouched in the corner and wept for shame, hating herself. Suddenly she cracked! Without warning, she ran for the door and headed for the deepest mineshaft, crying 'I'll never embarrass you again! I'll get out of your lives – permanently!' It was the classic melodrama! Catherine and George rushed after her, their anger suddenly dissolving in the night air. They caught up with her, in the words of the melodramas of the day, 'teetering on the edge of a black abyss – the dark, murky waters seeming to beckon her.' Suddenly, their anger spent, they both enveloped her in a bear hug. Cathy, now the caring mother, was the first to speak.

'OK, darling! It's all over now! Let's move on! We're on your side no matter what. We'll sort this out.'

George had the last word. 'I'll kill the bastard!'

They spent the morning planning redress. In the early afternoon, George scrambled on to old Naggy and set off for Clunes. He was chillingly calm and driven towards a just solution to this crisis. He knew where the Arblasters lived. But he did not personally know that 'useless oaf of a lying, conniving philanderer who had so shamed our daughter'. George hammered on the door. When Arthur through the window saw who it was, his smugness disappeared. The brats were off with their grandmother for the day. No answer. A firm shoulder sorted that out. George burst in. Not a soul to be seen. He began opening cupboards. Finally there was Arthur, hiding beneath his mother's petticoats. This had to be the perpetrator, this snivelling apology for a man, 'crouching under the frilly-laced underwear, guilt and fear etched into his erstwhile handsome face.'

At that moment, Mrs Arblaster entered the room, returning from her game of whist with the local ladies. She was totally aghast at the scene of this dishevelled, angry interloper towering over her son who crouched guiltily at the bottom of her wardrobe. She bravely lashed out with her umbrella. George parried the blow and snapped the umbrella in half. He put on his best English accent.

'I am sorry to intrude, Madame Arblaster. I am here to seek redress on behalf of my daughter, who has been raped by this snivelling bastard.'

'What daughter? You mean the chambermaid? What nonsense! Get out of my house! Help! Police!'

The police summarily arrived. What can a humble dirt-digger do against the upper crust Arblaster family and the Talbot legal fraternity?

'It was that shameless slut of yours who inveigled my son, tricked him, tempted him. What hot-blooded young man can resist such evil machinations? I will sue you and your family to within an inch of your life. Get out, now!'

The constable whispered, 'Yer better do wot she says. Yer 'aven't got a 'ope in 'ell!'

With wounded pride and a sense of injustice and a determination to balance the books, George returned home. All he said was:

'We have been stymied for the moment and seriously humiliated. It is not over yet!'

A week later, Arthur Arblaster was alighting from a coach after a riotous night with his friends. Two figures, armed with stringybark cudgels, emerged from the darkness. Systematically and wordlessly they proceeded to thrash Arthur to within an inch of his life. The perpetrators were never found. Of course, the chief suspects were the Kirby family. But they were at a neighbours' party as attested unanimously by the attending Stoney Creek farmers and their wives!

On cue the inevitable happened. Catherine had inherited her mother's level of fertility. Within three months she was 'showing'. There were the usual symptoms – cessation of periods, morning sickness, emotional outbursts.

George insisted on using the services of Dr Dowling of Amherst Hospital. With two weeks to go, the good doctor digitally checked the position of the baby. As we know, doctors then so frequently used unsterilised hands to handle corpses as well as living tissue. Catherine was suddenly seriously ill, suffering excruciating abdominal pain. In fact, she was at death's door. She was whisked off to hospital in the cart with John and George desperately flogging faithful old Naggy all the way to Amherst Hospital. They were too late. Three days later, on 8 June 1878, Catherine died of septicaemia.

Cathy and her children knew about death and funerals. Cathy, potato famine orphan, was closely acquainted with the loss of loved ones. She had thought it was all over. But it's never all over. The family wept unashamedly. It was all so totally unfair and unnecessary.

John wanted to return to the Arblaster home and administer another thrashing to that 'slimy Arthur Arblaster character'.

Cathy declared, 'What will that achieve?'

George added, 'That pitiless lot will know it is us. You'll finish in gaol. This time, we'll leave it to God to sort out.'

It was a private family funeral. There was no one there to judge her. She was one of their own, no matter what. So they kept their grief within the family.

It was the beginning of 1878 when a diphtheria epidemic appeared from nowhere. It targeted people of all ages, causing multiple deaths. Young children were particularly vulnerable. It was just after Christmas. Annie Kirby, now twenty-seven years of age, recognised within herself the symptoms of the dreaded disease. Annie was a healthy young woman unused to illness. Diphtheria proceeded to devastate the world over the next two years. It was a serious, highly contagious illness that attacks heart and nervous system. Was it water tank contamination again? Who knows? They all knew vaguely about contagious diseases. At the first sign of the symptoms, George whisked Annie off to the Amherst Hospital. They had got it in time. Mr Lyons claimed credit for her cure. Maybe it was just as much her general good health and strong constitution that made Annie one of the lucky survivors. After fourteen days she was on her way home. The official records triumphantly stated '… *CURED*'.

It is worth noting that if Annie, my great-grandmother, had not survived this life-threatening illness, this humble tome would not have seen the light of day.

As hospital accommodation was free for the working class, Annie had described herself as a domestic instead of a farmer's daughter. As we all know, she was a reliable and hard-working contributor to the market gardening activities of the Kirby family, which is as working class as you can get.

One month later, Elizabeth Kirby, Cathy's fourth daughter and Annie's younger sister, found herself in hospital afflicted by that same cruel disease. Like her older sister, she signed in as a domestic. The bad news is she spent forty-five days in hospital. The good news is that she was attended by the same Mr Lyons, who was credited with curing Annie. Most diphtheria victims in the 1870s did not survive. At the end of forty-five days, Mr Lyons declared Elizabeth '... *CURED*'.

The Stoney Creek School attended by Cathy and George's six children.

Ellen (Nelly) Sainsbery, Catherine's devoted grand-daughter, standing tall, left of the teacher, daughter of Lizzy and William, the dour Methodist blacksmith.

Annie Barrett – Catherine's sixth child and great-grandmother of Peter Hall, Margaret Walshe and Margaret Vrkljan.

James Edwin Barrett – Annie's husband and great-grandfather of Peter and the two Margarets.

Annie and James Edwin Barrett had six surviving children. The oldest was Eliza Barrett, here dressed up to the nines – Margaret Walshe's grandmother.

*The youngest of Annie and James' children was Kathleen Barrett (on the right),
Margaret Vrkljan's grandmother.*

*Alice Barrett, Peter Hall's grandmother, with her second husband, Sylvester Fitzpatrick,
and restless child Peter.*

*The formidable Sarah Lawson –
Catherine's thirteenth child.*

Sarah, with son Norman and Michael Hudson De Medeci, who died at Gallipoli.

Annie's house in Bond Street Talbot, which she shared with Ben, Lillah, and daughter Ellen.

The old Clunes Hospital where Catherine breathed her last.

The Amherst Cemetery, Catherine's final resting place.

Catherine's tombstone, set in place by Peter and the two Margarets.

She's Apples!

It is still 1878. Cathy, at forty-seven, was past her childbearing age, which meant that she could devote her undivided attention to the vegie garden. The last-born, baby Sarah, was two years of age. Her big brother John, at twenty-three, had become thoroughly adept in an impressive range of farming practices. He knew about dams, irrigation, gravity-fed water sources, windmills, cattle-buying, stock-breeding and feeding, the best kind of fodder, soil management and crop rotation, and he and George were thinking of starting an orchard. He left vegetable growing and harvesting to Cathy and the girls, but John and Naggie, their faithful old hack, ploughed the land to extend the vegie plot to three acres. Their two original bullocks, Bullo and Boris, had gone to God. It was Naggy who now dragged the rusty, second-hand plough-share through the unforgiving soil in preparation for another acre of vegetables.

They had been thinking of starting the orchard for some time. George had recently heard of a new crunchy but slightly tart eating apple that had become popular. A dear old lady, Marie Anna Smith, had chanced on a seedling that, as it grew to maturity, produced this green new tangy apple that became known as 'Granny Smith'. When

George crunched into his first Granny Smith, he knew that this was to be the chosen fruit for their orchard. He saved the pips and planted them. Nothing happened. By asking around, he soon learnt about the sophisticated process called 'grafting', which enabled you to grow healthy Granny Smith apple trees and successfully produce the tangy, crunchy fruit.

Sam Roxenburg, one of George's Protestant neighbours, was only too happy to share his expertise at grafting apple trees. Sam said it was best to do it the previous summer so that you are ready for planting the following spring. It was now the autumn of 1878. The process was far more sophisticated than dropping an apple pip into a hole in the ground. Sam spoke with the authority of the eighteenth century pedagogue he used to be.

'Are you ready and listening, my boy? OK! First you have to decide on a tough, disease-resistant stock, about three-eighth of an inch in diameter and with the root still intact at the bottom end. You cut the top of the stock at a wedge-shaped angle with a little hook on the end to prevent slippage. Next, you cut a corresponding angle on the bottom end of a cutting [called a 'scion'], obtained from a good fruiting variety. You then fit the stock and the cutting together, bind the graft firmly with string, and finally seal it with beeswax. Have you got all that?'

Sam's apple of choice was of course the new Granny Smith. Sam and George were on the same page. George followed the instructions to the letter and finished up with ten grafted baby apple trees ready for planting. He kept his lovingly grafted Granny Smiths in small temporary pots and scrupulously watered them every day.

'Don't flood them,' said Sam. 'Just keep them moist.' George was good at following instructions. By the beginning of spring, his grafted Granny Smiths were ready for planting.

John wanted to be involved. 'All you talk about, George, is Granny

Smith apples. Where do I fit in? If I'm gunna inherit this farm one day, I need to have my finger in every pie. How 'bout we do the apples together! You do the cattle, you do the market, and we'll do apples and ploughing together! Maybe we can swap next year.'

George's response was affirming. 'Good thinking, Johnny boy! You're going to be a great farmer one day. But don't get too excited. Remember I'm still the boss! And that pride goes before a fall!'

John had won the day. They did the apples together.

John had proved himself to have the makings of a hardworking and intelligent farmer. He was now more or less literate, thanks to stepfather George. Also there were fewer grammatical errors in his day-to-day conversation. John saw the farm as his birth-right, which meant that, as the oldest boy, he would inherit the property one day. This gave him the motivation to hang in there for the long haul and prove himself a worthy successor to the 'old man'.

George, stepfather, mentor and good mate, was essentially a fit and healthy fifty-five, though his hand had become slightly shaky, which was particularly obvious whenever he needed to sign his name on official documents. Looking at both the maths and the biology of their relationship, Cathy, seven years younger than George, was now forty-eight and past her childbearing age. In one sense she was quite pleased with her score of thirteen offspring, but being a superstitious Irishwoman she would have preferred a cast of twelve or fourteen.

Cathy was thought by the family to be invincible. The only time she saw anyone from the medical fraternity or sorority was when she was producing babies. She invariably performed her childbearing activities in style. She seemed a healthy specimen of Irish humanity. If you can survive the Irish Potato Famine, you can survive anything! Not entirely true! Cathy proved that she was as vulnerable as the rest of them.

We turn our attention on the Amherst Hospital records. We then focus on the most significant family member of the Kirby family – Catherine Kirby, our protagonist. It happened in March 1880. How dare she be flawed like the rest of us – becoming ill to the point of death. But the reality was that she was destined to do just that.

At forty-nine years of age, Cathy, mother of thirteen, was the driving force in the market garden venture. When she fell ill, lapsing into a coma, the invincible George was also beginning to fail. With the aid of John, he managed to carry Cathy to the cart. Cathy was not the lightweight she used to be. Off they went at a trot to their favoured hospital destination, Amherst – the panacea of all of their illnesses.

This time a new 'Mister', Mr Cavanagh, scratched his head. Cathy had come to – momentarily. The symptoms were puzzling – muscular weakness, aching joints, flaccidity, partial paralysis, throbbing headache, lapsing in and out of consciousness. Was this the dreaded botulism that can have its source in 'miasma' within the soil or rotten vegetables? Mr Cavanagh knew that botulism was a death sentence. He consulted Dr Dowling, but the good doctor was equally mystified. So they prescribed rest, hot broth, boiled potatoes, a tincture of iodine and fluid of magnesia. And hoped for the best.

A miracle occurred. Cathy started to recover. She slowly regained her strength. Her limbs began to move again. Her appetite returned. The headache subsided. Mr Cavanagh and Dr Dowling congratulated themselves and each other, without ever really knowing the nature of the mystery disease.

Two weeks later, 30 March 1880, Cathy returned to her vegies and her workforce as focused as ever.

'Come on you lot! No slacking!'

Maybe Cathy had simply been run down, after giving birth to and raising thirteen children. Then there was the death of daughter Catherine, and the daily grind working and managing a commercial enterprise. Be that as it may, Mr Cavanagh noted in the official hospital records:

'CATHERINE KIRBY ... CURED.'

These records are still available for perusal one hundred and fifty years later, despite the fact that the hospital, together with the rest of Amherst, was burned to the ground in 1985. One can imagine conscientious staff with wheelbarrows rescuing files as the hospital burnt around them. These patient files are all that is left of this historic goldfields hospital.

Life is all about births, deaths and marriages, at least that's what the official government statistics tell us. It was now time for two of Cathy's children to tie the knot.

Margaret was the first to embark on the married state, which according to official records happened on 7 August 1876. She was eighteen years of age and couldn't wait to find that perfect, kind, gentle man. From her earliest days she wanted nothing more than to be cuddled and loved. There was no better way for that to happen than within a good marriage. Nathaniel Hocking was the lucky man. But it was bad luck for the vegie garden, for it meant that Cathy would lose one of her best workers. We don't have any subsequent details about her marriage. Let's hope she lived happily ever after. She deserved nothing but the best.

Annie was next ...

Annie Ties the Knot

Six years later, it was Annie's turn. At seventeen, she was sick of potatoes, turnips and carrots. She felt that there must be more to life than digging, planting, lugging buckets of water and carting cow dung. One delightfully fine summer's day, Cathy entrusted to her the prized Talbot Market job.

Imagine Annie standing confidently behind a stall laden with potatoes and sundry other vegetables. She was in full sail, spruiking her wares in her shrill soprano voice. She caught the eye of a tall, gangly miner who winked at her. She blushed, looked down at her potatoes, looked up again, half-smiled and winked back. Then she remembered that young girls don't wink at strangers.

Annie was conflicted between embarrassment and elation. She reverted to her salesgirl role, offering him a large, healthy-looking potato.

'Taters at a penny a pound, sir, fresh from my ma's market garden this morning, but you can have that one for free.'

The young man bit into the potato and declared, 'I prefer my spuds cooked. How about you cook it for me!'

More conflicted than ever, Annie responded, 'But I've got to work!'

The miner's response was, 'Fair enough! Work now. We'll catch up after work. You finish at four. I'll see you then – outside the Presbyterian church!'

Her miner disappeared into the crowd.

Annie continued to be confused and elated. How could anyone fall for a plain face like hers? Whenever she looked in the mirror she saw a bland, ordinary face. But that's not how others saw her. In fact she was quite a beauty.

Big brother John arrived at four o'clock with horse and cart to pick up the table, the wares and the till.

'Well done, Annie. We'll make a salesgirl out of you yet!'

'Thanks John! See you later. I'm off to meet someone special.' She disappeared into the crowd.

They sat under a tree beside the graveyard behind the church. Just like her sister Margaret, it was love at first sight. He would indeed do! They subtly cross-examined each other over the next two hours. James was a twenty-year-old miner from Chinaman's Flat.

'What's more, I've struck it rich', he boasted. To prove his credentials, he produced a minute gold nugget from a sow's ear purse snuggling safely within the depths of his voluminous pants pocket.

'Wow! You must be rich!' responded innocent young Annie. His full name was James Edwin Barrett II. 'What a classy name!'

He hadn't finished yet. 'And, furthermore, my dad, James Edwin Barrett I, was an opera singer. Beat that!'

Annie couldn't beat that. She responded forlornly, 'All we've got is fifteen cattle and a market garden.'

'Sounds good to me!' responded James Edwin. 'I reckon we're made for each other.' He still hadn't finished yet. 'What's more, just like my dad, our family is Presbyterian, not like those riff-raff Roman Catholics you see everywhere.'

Whoops! Suddenly Annie took a step back, declaring acerbically.

'Hold it there! My family are Australian Catholics and proud of it! We are not Roman Catholics. No way did we come from Rome, wherever that is.' He had struck a raw nerve. 'And what's more, Presbyterians are Proddies like the Anglicans that killed off my mother's family by starving them to death during the Potato Famine!' Edwin, realising he had put his foot in it, quickly added:

'Of course there are bad Protestants as well as good Catholics. I'm sure you're one of the good ones. I apologise!'

Mollified, she conceded, 'That's OK. My step-dad is a Protestant. And he's one of the good ones.' Despite the blip, Annie felt that this was maybe what 'falling in love' was about.

There we have it – James Edwin Barrett II – gold miner, six feet tall, healthy self-image, tolerably handsome. Annie – inexperienced in the ways of the world, impressionable, brown eyes, long flowing black locks and, if she only knew it, a serious contender for the annual Talbot Beauty Pageant.

How was the love affair viewed by the family? First, Cathy was convinced by past experience that, in her role as mother of a prospective bride-to-be, she had to check on the spouse's credentials. At the time, George was feeling poorly and confined to bed and therefore missed out on the interrogation. This prospective husband, James, was a miner just like her first husband James. So far so good! But, even more so than Annie, she was concerned when she heard that he was a Protestant, a Presbyterian in fact, which for Cathy was not quite as bad as Church of England, but all the same was bad enough. He would have to be very good in other ways if he were to match her exacting standards. Maybe he was a good Proddy, like her dear husband George.

James Barrett explained: 'Presbyterianism came from Scotland, and the Scots came from the Celts, just as the Irish did.'

'So far, so good! How about your family history?'

'My dad, James Edwin Barrett I, came from Ireland, where he had been an opera baritone, and what's more I have inherited some of his talent as a singer.'

Cathy responded, 'Demonstrate!'

So he did, with '*Funiculi, funicula*'.

'That's enough! declared Cathy. 'Opera is not my thing. I suppose you'll do, providing you promise to look after our Annie.'

Naturally George approved. The prospect of introducing more Protestant blood into the family seemed like a marvellous idea, although he had previously thought that Presbyterians were rather dour and excessively serious about the place of God in their lives. But this particular Presbyterian was fond of a laugh and indeed ticked most boxes.

'He'll do fine!' declared George.

It was time for the family to meet this newcomer. When the day arrived for the inter-family gathering, specially designed for assessing potential in-laws, Cathy insisted that the prospective father-in-law, James Edwin Barrett I, demonstrate his vocal expertise. 'Maybe a party kind of song!' Being piano-less they didn't have any ivories to tickle, but J. E. Barrett I, with a glass of beer in his hand, launched into *Libiamo ne'lieti*, the drinking song from *La Traviata*. At the end of the song, everyone clapped politely. Except Cathy!

She couldn't resist sharing her real sentiments. 'I'm sure that was really good. But I don't know that one. How about something more toe-tapping like *Wearing of the Green?*'

James Edwin Senior *did* in fact know that one, but he couldn't bring himself to express such pro-Irish-Catholic and therefore anti-British sentiments. The lines about 'hanging men and women for the wearing of the green' were uncomfortable for a Presbyterian to sing about.

He countered with, 'I'm a bit rusty on that one! How about *Danny Boy?*'

They all agreed except for Cathy who wanted *Wearing of the Green* or nothing. She went off into the kitchen to pour more beer for the guests and Granny Smith apple juice for the children. Soon both families were lustily pumping out the song about Danny Boy and the calling pipes, and wept into their beer and apple juice when they came to the colleen who had departed this world.

Annie and James Edwin's wedding was attended by a motley collection of family and friends – an admixture of Protestants and Catholics – who were willing and able to complete the arduous thirty mile journey from Talbot to Ballarat. They arrived at St Andrew's Free Presbyterian church by coach or on horseback. Cathy had come to terms with the idea of a non-Catholic wedding by convincing herself that the Scots and the Catholics were on the same side against the English. Nevertheless, she was disappointed that there was no sermon with funny jokes, no laughter, no incense, no ringing of bells and no words of consecration like in a *real* Catholic Mass. But Reverend William Henderson seemed like a nice chap and knew what he was doing. She consoled herself with the certainty that, unlike herself and George, Annie and James were really married in the eyes of the world and maybe God too.

After the wedding, James Edwin and Annie returned to Chinaman's Flat. There they lived frugally in a tent among the Chinese. Unfortunately for them, the only ones to strike it rich were the hardworking Chinese, who read the topography with oriental expertise and somehow like homing pigeons were able to pinpoint the gold-bearing deposits. Annie and James Edwin, despite their best efforts, couldn't compete. After six fruitless months, they had to accept the humiliating alternative of returning to Talbot where James Edwin became a farm labourer and Annie a housemaid. James Edwin, the erstwhile ambitious goldminer, was for the moment too proud to ask for work on the Kirby/Lawson farm.

To complicate matters, Annie discovered she was pregnant. It was good news and bad news. The good news was that it heralded the beginning of Annie's dream of having a family to match her mother's. The bad news was they were so poor that they could not afford to sustain their independence. It meant the humiliation of returning to the farm and begging for work and accommodation. But it was not entirely bad news because George was now too sick to work and they needed an extra farmhand. And Cathy had been missing her daughter Annie, so she was thrilled at the prospect of having Annie back and a new baby in the house.

Finally, eating humble pie, they returned home to work in the vegie garden, despite James Edwin's conviction that gardening was for girls. But he quickly adapted. He was a hard worker, having developed a good work ethic in the mines, and he was a quick learner. After an apprenticeship watering vegetables, digging out weeds and extracting potatoes from the unforgiving soil, he was promoted to working with William and Johnny, chopping, digging, carting, ploughing, attending to the orchard and taking his turn at selling produce at the Talbot market. Johnny was in charge of the orchard, which now boasted forty Granny Smith apple trees – the number-one market favourite. The three boys got on well as long as the two underlings recognised Johnny as the boss.

In 1881, Eliza Mabel saw the light of day. James Edwin had studied the statistics on hospital births and insisted on home birthing. It came about under the sure hand of midwife Rachel O'Grady. Eliza Mabel had wispy strands of brownish hair, just like her father.

James Edwin declared proudly, 'I must say she's rather perfect – just like me.'

Annie chipped in: 'She is indeed a fantastically beautiful baby, with brown eyes – just like me.'

James Edwin had to concede, 'Maybe she's got the best of both worlds.'

*In our story, Eliza Mabel was the first of the three female offspring
who made this story possible. The three protagonists who did the
delving into the life of Cathy the potato famine orphan were Margaret
Vrkljam, the initiator, Margaret Walshe, the investigator and grand-
daughter of Eliza Mabel, and myself, Peter Hall, the storyteller, who
embellished as he deemed appropriate. Catherine was our great-great-
grandmother, and her daughter Annie was our great-grandmother.
On with the story!*

They celebrated with Granny Smith apple cider for all the family, except for Eliza Mabel, who preferred mother's milk. But there was never
enough of it! For some reason, Annie produced insufficient milk to sat-
isfy the cravings of her newborn, which meant she had to resort to cow's
milk and the tried and true cow-horn system. Eliza quickly made the
transition. She was soon expanding in all directions and gooing affably
at her adoring aunts and uncles, not to mention Mum, Dad and Gran.

No sooner was Annie back on the vegies than the now familiar
symptoms began to reoccur.

'Good news, J.E. I think I'm preggers again!'

J.E., as they now all called him, shouted excitedly, 'Whoopee! Atta
girl!'

Her fertility was certainly not in question. Seven months later Annie had to resign from her gardening job. Her abdomen bulged dramatically. She waddled around the house 'like an egg-bound duck' [as my
father Cliff used to say affectionately of my mother Amy].

Six weeks to go, midwife Rachel O'Grady, pronounced her progno-
sis – 'Twins, it is! And they want to pop out right now! I can't handle six
weeks prem. It's off to Amherst Hospital with yer!'

The pain was excruciating! 'I've changed my mind. One's enough!'
wailed Annie.

'Too late, love! They're on the way,' declared Nurse Croucher.
'Scream as much as you like, and bite on this clothes peg.'

Two hours later one skinny, undersized gremlin slid out, and two minutes later, a second one. Twin boys! They both looked so wretchedly weak and puny.

'I'm sorry, love. I don't like their chances.'

'Rubbish!' retorted Annie defiantly. 'I'm their mum. I'll look after them, and they're going to be fine!'

But they weren't fine. Two days later, newborn Edward succumbed. Father James Edwin lost his habitual cool and sobbed inconsolably in Annie's arms. Annie choked back her tears and reassured him, 'Maybe it was meant to be, love. At least we still have little James!'

Nine days later, little James also slipped away. James Edwin was the strong one this time.

'My Presbyterian mum and dad would tell me it's God's will.'

Annie was out of control in her grief. 'I don't believe that bullshit!' she responded. 'If there's a God, how could he allow two sweet innocent babes to die like that?' James Edwin had no answer. He simply held her more tightly.

George continued to lose weight and physical strength. He suffered from abdominal bloating, recurring fever, and his complexion had taken on a yellowish hue. He was used to being the invincible one. It was he who insisted on sending other ailing members of the family to Amherst Hospital whenever his home-grown diagnostic expertise deemed it necessary. He thought of himself as the iron man, the invincible carer of the family. But now it was his turn. It was pride that made George reluctant to confront the medical fraternity at Amherst. Despite the success of this noble institution, he had never quite got over the sad death of stepdaughter Catherine. Instead, whenever he deemed it necessary, he decided to commit himself to the care of the newly constructed hospital at Clunes, which was beginning to develop a good reputation. For the moment he decided to put off the evil day.

Cathy was now running the house and the business. George looked ten years older than his fifty-seven years. He walked like an old man, had become very feeble, and spent most of the day in bed. It was time!

John, with George bouncing uncomfortably in the back, made his way in the old cart drawn by the faithful Naggy to the new Clunes Hospital. Predictably, George was diagnosed with liver cancer. Everyone knew that liver cancer was a fatal disease. It was just a matter of time.

Monday to Friday, Sarah, Mary, Ben and Martha left home for school at 8.00 o'clock. They usually walked the two miles to school within forty minutes. They were all slim, trim and fit like their parents. They lugged school bags containing reader, exercise book, ruler, slate pencil and sponge-in-a-tin, together with two stale bread-and-dripping sandwiches.

The years raced by. It was now 1882. All of Cathy and George's six young children were either attending Stoney Creek Primary School or had now graduated. Sarah now six was in Grade 1, Mary in Grade 3, Ben in Grade 5, and Martha in Grade 7. William and Eliza Jane had left school and joined the market garden contingent, consisting of Cathy, Elizabeth, Annie and Ellen.

On the way to school, Ben and his mates overtook the dawdlers, engaging in typical schoolboy banter, scuffles and the occasional full-on stoush. The girls were less physical, restricting themselves to name-calling, teasing, preening and chatting. Aggressive behaviour was the exception. Most of the time they all got on well.

Mr James Knight was the head teacher and, to begin with, the only teacher. He was strict but fair. Talking in class was a serious breach of discipline, the consequence being the application of the cane to the rear end for boys or on the hand for girls.

'Spare the rod and spoil the child,' he often proclaimed to anyone who was prepared to listen.

Most of the parents declared their wholehearted agreement. Benjamin had his own views on corporal punishment.

'If boys get it on the bum, it should be the same for girls!' He was obviously before his time, being an advocate of gender equality! Margaret, Annie and Ellen didn't agree.

'Boys are much naughtier than girls, so they deserve it!'

They had become quite adept in reading, writing and 'rithmetic (taught to the tune of a hickory stick!). They respected their teacher, laughed at his jokes, and lustily sang 'God save the King' at his bidding.

As George was the education and health aficionado, they were known as the *Lawson kids* in the context of both school and hospital. For Cathy, who saw herself as the main player in making them and bringing them into the world, they were *Kirbys*. Their birth certificates proved it.

18

Suddenly Lawsons

The following year, George and Cathy's children really became Lawsons, as did Cathy. George's health had deteriorated significantly since the middle of 1882. He was admitted to the new Clunes Hospital. His symptoms were mainly loss of weight and appetite, nausea and pressure under his ribs, on the right side. It was most certainly cancer of the liver – a death sentence, as he already expected. Ever the stoic Englishman, he chose to remain at home as long as possible. He continued to smile his whimsical smile. He never complained.

It was Friday 1 June 1883. George was fifty-eight years of age, far in excess of the average life expectancy of forty at that time. He knew that he was about to go to God. He knew that he had been living in sin, having cohabited with Cathy for seventeen years. He had brought six children into this world, all without God's blessing. Before he left them, he had to do something about it. They needed to get properly married.

They still could not agree on the Catholic-Protestant dilemma. So they chose neutral territory – the Bible Christian Church. The American pastor, Reverend William Bitten of the said newly founded church performed the ceremony. George and Catherine were officially man and wife. They were now proudly to be known as Lawsons, in all contexts. George was ready to go to his God, absolved of his sins.

They were all there in the new Clunes Hospital – the Kirbys and the Lawsons. It was a modern hospital, even if it was smaller than the neighbouring Amherst one. It had been built a mere ten years ago, funded by gold. They stood stoically beside his bed, because they thought that was how George wanted it.

'None of that weeping and wailing! Stiff upper lip! Understood?'

Biting her lip, twenty-two-year-old Annie responded, 'We'll try our best … Father!' The others simply nodded.

That's how it is with liver cancer. George became quite eloquent in his dying moments.

'The pain … is tolerable', he said. He summoned up a last bit of energy for a speech of a lifetime. 'But I'm going to miss you all … Life is a roll of the dice. When it's time, you go down smiling. Shed a few tears. Remember me! Work hard! Look after your mum and each other! And above all … be good!' They were struggling.

'All of you, give me a hug! Remember … I'm still in charge!

'Catherine first, then all of you in order of age. Cathy, my darling wife! You're the best thing that's happened to me in my all too brief life. It reminds me of that line from *Macbeth*, "Out, brief candle!"

'Johnny, my cheeky work-mate! Shake my hand and, if it's not too unmanly, give me a hug.

'My gentle Margy. I hope Nat's treating you well. If not, I'll …

'And my bubbly Lizzy, stay happy and keep bubbling!

'Annie and James, keep the home fires burning. Give baby Eliza a cuddle from me.

'Ellen, the last but not least of James' daughters, you're a credit to him. I'll say "hello" for you when I meet him.

'And my lot! Thanks again, Cathy, for your part in bringing them into the world. Just remember that without me you couldn't have done it!

'Eliza Jane, you're the first of the Lawson kids and the first to learn reading, writing and arithmetic. I'm so proud of you.

'Willy, you're fourteen now – a young man. I'm thrilled to whatever back teeth I still have that you and John are such mates. Stay that way.

'Martha, I saw you making eyes at David Henson last week. He's a fine fellow. I'd like to be here to see what happens.

'Benjamin, my youngest son, stand up for yourself. Don't let anyone bully you, particularly big brother Willy.

'Mary, happy birthday for next week! I'll say hello to Jesus' mother for you when I see her.

'And, last but not least, little Sarah. How's Grade 1 going? They say we keep the best to last.

'That's it, family. I'm feeling pretty weak. I'm out of puff. I'll rest now ...'

George was indeed weak but entirely lucid. He had said his piece with all the eloquence he could muster. The symptoms were there – fever, weakness and a yellow complexion. The end was predictable. Soon he drifted into unconsciousness, shuddered slightly and it was all over.

George was buried in an unmarked grave at the Clunes Cemetery just like his predecessor, James. Following the Kirby tradition, the family placed on the grave a small wooden cross, cobbled up by John, with name, dates of birth and death, and a simple RIP. Nature disposed of the cross in the ensuing years, and it was left to his inquisitive ancestors to unravel the mysteries that George carried with him to eternity.

Life without George

Polonius informs us that, 'Brevity is the soul of wit.' So let us be brief for the rest of our story.

The farm continued to be the thing. John was twenty-nine, and according to George's legacy was legally in charge. Catherine was now an active fifty-two and still the power behind the throne. The market garden continued to thrive, as did the Granny Smith orchard and the beef cattle program. They survived flood, fire and drought, and despite minor disagreements, they sorted out disputes amicably. One by one, they departed the farm sometimes in a box, but usually in search of pastures new, such as marriage, new occupation or different lifestyle.

Usually, Cathy stood back and left John to make the decisions. But, whenever she believed he had it wrong, she intervened with sage maternal advice. John was less feisty these days. The farm thrived, their water source continued to work, the vegetables continued to reproduce, selling at cut-price rates to match the Chinese, the herd of mainly beef cattle was kept at fifteen – most of them steers, destined for the butcher-shop. The pièce de résistance was definitely the Granny Smiths, which were as popular as ever at the Talbot market.

The market garden was in the capable hands of Cathy, as supervisor. The workforce included Lizzy, twenty-four, Ellen, twenty-one, Martha, fourteen, and, for the moment, Annie, twenty-three. They made a formidable team. Manpower, as distinct from womanpower, included Johnny, thirty, as boss assisted by Will, fourteen, and, temporarily, James Edwin, twenty-five, the affable, hard-working jokester and husband to Annie.

Despite his Presbyterian background, J.E. kept the boys entertained with his endless repertoire of blue jokes, of which Willy was frequently the victim. He kept reminding them that his name was William. They took no notice but continued to tease him with 'willy' jokes. William decided that the best ploy was to laugh it off, occasionally throwing in a Johnno and Jimbo gag of his own, which usually fell flat.

J.E. was restless. He did not want to be forever beholden to others. He was grateful to Annie and the family for making him welcome within their family enterprise. He was more than convinced that the market garden and cattle business were a good family investment. But this was Annie's family, not his. He did not want to piggyback on their success. It was time to get out.

Cathy, who didn't trust banks, had a good stash of paper notes hidden in a box under the house. She didn't tell the children about her secret, but they all knew about mum's treasure chest. Being scrupulously honest, there was no way they would violate her trust. The 'rainy day' had arrived. One day, Cathy summoned Annie and J.E. to her boudoir.

'The contents of this tin are yours. Use it wisely. Get yourself a property, not too far away, and set yourselves up. Pay it back when you can, because the treasure trove is to share amongst all of us.'

Annie's vision suddenly became blurry as she struggled to hold back the tears. The Lawsons usually tried not to get soppy about good deeds. All she could manage was:

'Thanks ever so much, Ma.'

James Edwin had a gigantic lump in his throat. He was totally conflicted between, 'No thanks, we treasure our independence', and, 'You beauty, darling mother-in-law! We'll look after you in style in your old age.'

Finally, he simply said, 'Thanks Mrs Lawson. We won't let you down! You'll have it back with interest in no time.'

'Forget about the interest. Use it wisely, and when you're able we'll pop it back in the coffers for the next family emergency. And by the way, forget about that Mrs Lawson stuff. It's Cathy, or Catherine if you want to be poncy about it. OK?'

Twelve months later they received their first rates notice. Fortunately they were able to pay on time, and continued to do so in years to come as council records attest.

J.E. was now a farmer. Farmer Barrett had a certain ring about it. He had learnt the trade from Cathy and Johnny. The property was three miles away – twenty acres on the outskirts of Talbot. They saw themselves fortunate to have a rambling old farmhouse, a shed, a reel of barbed wire, and a stash of tools bequeathed by Farmer Giles, the previous incumbent. Like the Kirby/Lawsons he decided to diversify. Within two years, they had a half-dozen cows, ten lambs, a half-acre of cabbages, turnips, carrots and spuds, a plot set aside for fruit trees, and a large mortgage. It wasn't a mortgage in the ordinary sense. It was the loan from Cathy which he was paying back progressively despite her protestations. They were determined to turn it into a profitable enterprise.

They were lucky to be close to the Talbot market. Annie just loved cherries, so cherries it was – an acre of cherry trees to start with. J.E. totally approved, but added, 'Maybe we'll do Granny Smiths like yer ma in a few years' time.'

The years continued to click over – inexorably. It is now 1884. As they sat perusing the rates notice, Annie looked optimistically at her bulging midriff. She was now full term.

'We'll be right this time, love.'

J.E.'s response was cryptic. 'You betcha!'

WILLIAM, named after his uncle Willy, emerged quite painlessly two days later. Eliza Mabel squealed with delight when she first saw her baby brother, who looked healthy despite his blue colour. Annie and James-Edwin were puzzled by the bluish tinge on their otherwise healthy newborn. Still grieving over the loss of the twins, they went immediately to consult their favourite barber-surgeon, Mr Lyons, of Amherst Hospital fame. They were devastated when he handed over his verdict.

'William appears to be suffering from blue baby syndrome.'

Annie didn't understand.

'What's that mean? Is it serious?'

The worthy Mr Lyons responded:

'Blue baby syndrome is a condition probably caused by nitrate contamination in the groundwater of your property. We must wait and hope for the best.'

They immediately contacted the previous owner. He assured them in no uncertain terms:

'We have never used nitrate fertiliser on that property. Our own five children, who were born there, have always been as healthy as you could hope for. We are sorry for your son. But don't blame us!' End of story!

Meanwhile little William, his blood starved of oxygen, continued to fail. The blueness persisted. James Edwin and Annie once again took their little blue baby to Amherst Hospital hoping for a miracle. Surely Mr Lyons could work his magic and turn that blueness to a healthy pink. He was most sympathetic about the plight of one of his favourite patients.

'I'm terribly sorry for both of you. It appears that oxygen is not reaching the blood. There is a problem with the heart's pumping system.

Your baby's blood is not being oxygenated. Hence the blue colour. All we can do is pray that it's a problem that will correct itself.'

It didn't correct itself. William became weaker as the days went by. He passed away painlessly at ten weeks.

James Edwin and Annie were utterly shattered by the death of a third newborn. How could you lose three beautiful babies in three years? What had they done to deserve this devastating outcome? Was God punishing them a third time for some misdemeanour? Was it because Annie had insulted her God by marrying a Protestant in a Protestant church?

'No way!' said James Edwin with conviction. 'Didn't Ruth in the Bible say, "Your God is my God"?' Annie had no answer.

'Maybe that's it! Maybe we shouldn't try for any more babies. Obviously God's out to get us!'

'No sweet pea! We are not giving up! As an ex-miner, I know about the betting game. There is such a thing as a run of good luck followed by a run of bad luck. If you hang in there, the tables will turn. We are not going to give up!'

And the tables did turn! ALICE MAUDE joined the human race the following year, 1885. Alice Maude Barrett began her life as a chubby eight-pounder and right from the start was a ball of energy. One of her first skills was learning how to smile. She moved from smile to giggle to full-on laughter. She would lie on her back and kick like a mule. She laughed like a hyena and learned to gurgle then gargle in the first year, to the mirth of the whole family. She would gargle endlessly till she ran out of breath. Soon she was dragging herself crab-like over the splintery floor. Splinters meant tears, which never lasted long. James was forever on his knees removing wayward splinters from the rough hardwood floors. Alice gradually learned her lesson when yet another splinter embedded itself into either her leg or worse still her bottom. It was time to vary her method of propulsion. Learning to walk was a better option.

At two Alice still refused to play by the rules and was expert at tip-ping over vases, saucepans and the chamber-pot, all of which to her was part of the game and which caused her to laugh uproariously. She was a slow learner, despite sundry smacks on the bottom administered by mother Annie.

Alice was quite a tomboy, but a lovable, rollicking and a supremely affectionate one. Soon she was to add another endearing quality to her repertoire when newborn Annie Myrtle graced the scene in 1888. Alice then took on the little mother role, cooing, cuddling, endlessly singing *Rock-a-bye Baby* and *Twinkle, Twinkle* in her loud, abrasive voice. Having two Annies in the one house was confusing and so Annie Myrtle soon became simply Myrtle.

The three sisters were healthy and fit and survived sisterly interaction despite their differing personalities. Eliza was slim, serious, prim, proper and bossy. Alice was loud, raucous, quirky, and had a will of her own. Myrtle was calm, easy-going and looked up adoringly to her two elder sisters. The three-year age difference helped them to accept rather than challenge each other, interacting protectively with their siblings rather than treating them as rivals.

James Edwin and Annie Barrett now had child-producing expertise down pat. They had contributed three delightfully diverse and healthy girls to their repertoire. It was time for an injection of masculinity into the Barrett progeny. In 1890 WILLIAM JAMES came into existence. Being the first boy, Little Billy was spoilt rotten by his adoring sisters. Having lost their blue baby William six years ago, they wanted to remember him somehow. They were conflicted about names and hesitated about putting a mozz on the little fellow, so William quickly became Little Billy.

The year 1892 saw the birth of yet another boy, EDWIN. As for most people of that era, family names were important, particularly given that life was so fragile with multiple diseases lurking around the corner ready to strike. J.E., coming from a family where retaining traditional family names was important, couldn't let his second son enter this world without bequeathing to him at least half his name. Individuality was not as important in those days. Compare such modern once-off names like Cosmo, Colt and Congo!

Three years later, James Edwin and Annie's ninth and last child came into existence – KATHLEEN ISABELLA. Annie was now thirty-one. For some reason, whether it be a parental decision or nature's way of declaring enough's enough, Kathleen Isabella was to be the last of the surviving six.

Kathleen Isabella is of special significance in our story. Without her these pages would never have been penned. She was the great-grand-mother of the initiator of the research into our story, Margaret Vrkljan.

Kathleen Isabella, the fourth girl, was born in 1895. From her first breath, she was a calm, gentle baby exuding peace and tranquillity. No blood-curdling screams or temper tantrums – just dove-like cooing at feeding time. For the first month Annie was on tap every four hours per-forming her mother-role as purveyor of life-sustaining milk. Between times she was back on the vegies.

Four girls, two boys! The gender imbalance was apparently God's will for the Barrett family. Or was there some mysterious, more scien-tific, genetic explanation? Why did girls predominate amongst the sur-vivors within the Kirby/Lawson/Barrett families? There are all kinds of old wives' tales as well as medically based theories about sex determina-tion. J.E. was not interested in whys and wherefores. For him the main issue was having sons to till and inherit the land. Whew! He now had two sons on whom he could depend to take over the farm one day. One of the two could be a doctor or a candlestick-maker if he so wished, pro-vided the other was prepared to run the farm.

Between times, Annie continued to work on the vegie garden with husband J.E., the tough, hard-working ex-miner now tiller of the land. The girls at fourteen, ten and seven, were expected to put in an hour each day after school weeding and watering, together with a few extra hours in the weekend. There was still time for skippy, hoppy, hidey and cavorting with baby Katy. Billy and Ed, at five and three respectively, tried to join in the games, which they usually wrecked by breaking the rules, sometimes accidentally sometimes intentionally. When they became bored they threw stones at jam tins (which had now been invented) or wrestled amicably in the long grass behind the house. Assuredly, boys would forever be boys!

Fourteen-year-old Eliza, as bossy as ever, competed with ten-year-old Alice in spoiling young Katy, who continued to be the perfect unflappable little lady, until she reached the magic age of two. It was then that she began to spread her wings, learning how to get her own way using her newly acquired skill of stubborn determination.

'That's my dolly. Don't touch it! It's mine!'

'You've got to learn to share, Katy!'

'I don't want to share. It's my dolly.'

She had learnt that possession is nine-tenths of the law. She expressed this view quite simply with, 'It's mine!' She learnt how to win the tug-of-war. Scratch, scream and pull hair and you've won.

It is fascinating how we experiment with different personas [*personae*] as we grow up. By the time she reached three, she returned to the calm, sharing, happy little girl that was the real Lizzy. It worked better than 'aggro'.

Meanwhile, at twelve, Alice wasn't interested in pretty clothes and girly toys. She was a tomboy except for one thing. From her earliest days she was obsessed by food and how to turn the simplest ingredients into a culinary delight. She would gather twigs from the surrounding bush, stack them inside the old woodstove, strike a match, and soon the fire would be crackling energetically, fanned by a blast of air from the bottom vent. Roast potatoes were her speciality – golden and crunchy on the outside, soft and creamy on the inside – a food connoisseur's delight.

In her nineties, Alice's specialty was still her magic roast potatoes cooked in the old woodstove in her dilapidated Northcote home. Her Northcote kitchen had a dirt floor with a smooth shiny black surface, created over the years by splashes of grease from innumerable baking episodes. For us kids, it was 'Yum, yum, crunchy roast spuds!' – the ultimate gastronomic delight. Annie Kirby would have been proud of her. I can still remember the raucous laugh, the deep gravelly voice, the laughing eyes, the portly figure in a long black dress, rocking from side to side as she waddled around in the dim light of the grimy kitchen.

Staying healthy in the 1880s and '90s was serious business. Fortunately, medicine had taken a significant step forwards with the discovery of disease-bearing germs. This new medical breakthrough had to compete with the commonly accepted miasma theory, which blamed bad air as the prime cause of disease. Germ theory was soon generally accepted, leading to improved hygiene and the disinfecting of hands. The term 'germ' was the pseudo-medical term for organisms that caused infection. 'Germs' soon morphed into the more generally accepted medical term 'bacteria', which included all micro-organisms, good and bad. Whatever terminology you used, the discovery of these two concepts led to a dramatic reduction in infection. The result was increased survival rates in hospitals, which had hitherto been perfect environments for the spread of bacteria. Improved cleanliness, use of heat to kill bacteria, chemical disinfection, and new medications dramatically improved survival statistics in hospitals, which too often in the past had been hotbeds of infection.

At the same time, Edward Jenner's contribution to the understanding of cowpox and smallpox diseases was gradually taken on board. The medical confraternity was stubborn and slow to accept new ways. Invasive processes like inoculation were not immediately implemented, hence the smallpox epidemic of 1881-1882. It took time to accept the concept of inoculating with cowpox to give immunity to smallpox, a once deadly disease. This marked the beginning of sophisticated medical solutions for common diseases.

Joseph Lister's theory on sanitation and hand washing before operations was initially viewed with scepticism, before being tentatively implemented by the medical fraternity. For many of them, if it looked clean, it was clean. The theory about germs that you can't see was hard for them to swallow. They took it as an attack on their professionalism and age-old medical traditions. There were many common diseases, with solutions that we take for granted nowadays, which in the late 1800s were still not understood. Diphtheria, cholera, typhoid, tuberculosis, polio, measles and mumps continued to elude the medical fraternity.

James Edwin and Annie Barrett had never really come to terms with the deaths of their second, third and fourth children – James, Edward and William. Fortunately, the six surviving children were fit and healthy and growing up fast. By the turn of the century, we now have Eliza Mabel, nineteen, Alice Maud, fifteen, Annie Myrtle, twelve, William James ten, Edwin, eight, and Kathleen Isabella, five. Key players in our story are to be ELIZA MABEL, ALICE MAUDE and KATHLEEN ISABELLA.

The main contributors to the researching and the telling of this tale are Margaret Vrkljan, Margaret Walshe and Peter Hall – descendants respectively of Kathleen Isabella, Eliza Mabel and Alice Maude.

Turn of the Century

By the year 1900, Grandma Cathy was a hale and hearty sixty-eight. For Cathy it was an era of bewildering changes – scientific advances, social upheaval and the impending threat of a world war. The twentieth century was the era of technology, a burgeoning population, universal education, and sophisticated scientific and medical advances. Electric and electronic devices were on the cusp of becoming universally available. There were new and sophisticated ways of moving from A to B – everything from the pushbike to the motorcar. We now had ice-cream cones and paper towels, Herbert Johnson's electric mixer and the zip fastener.

Cathy was aware of those new noisy, motorised devices for carrying the well-heeled. By 1914, Henry Ford's first assembly line was to produce the motorcar in large numbers and at a price that many households could afford. For Cathy it was a question of seeing and not possessing. She would never have been able to afford a motorcar, nor would she have wanted one. A motorcar could never match the warm, living, breathing, functional companionship of good old Naggy.

New methods of mass destruction as well as air travel were in the wind. There were dirigibles floating through the skies, music emanating from boxes called phonographs. Cathy and her family were very much working class and could not keep up with these new innovations. Nor could they afford them. During her final fourteen years Cathy was vaguely aware of these innovations. But her main focus was family and how to survive.

At the turn of the century Cathy, now sixty-eight, decided it was time to move out and leave the house and the management of the farm to her children. As long as she stayed there, she couldn't resist bossing them around. They needed their independence as she herself did.

John continued to be very much in charge at the farm. Willy and his family were happy with the balance of power. After all, they had the house – perfect for wife Emily and their four boisterous kids, aged from two to eight. In return, Will was meekly at Johnny's beck and call, working assiduously ten hours a day, five and a half days a week. A perfect arrangement!

John was totally content with his folksy wattle and daub cabin. He loved his independence, his cosy bed, his homemade rustic table and rickety chairs, his personally designed kerosene-tin washbasin, with a pipe from the water-tank to supply water to his cosy abode. Minimal housework! Perfect for a bachelor! Company when he felt like it! His little bit of luxury was dining with the family at the end of a long day.

The outhouse was common property, now less noisome than back in '65. A wooden lid with boot-leather hinges kept the flies out. Each year, they dug a new six-foot pit. It was all hands on deck, which meant two stalwart men, one woman and four little kids. They shoved and shuffled the outhouse over planks, skidding it over to the newly prepared hole.

As if on cue, little Josh fell into it. They lowered eight-year-old Seth headfirst down the hole with Johnny hanging on to his legs. Seth grabbed Josh by his shirt and tried to drag him screaming to the surface, with Johnny yelling:

'Come on, you lot. I've got 'em both. But who's got me?' They all grabbed arms, shoulders and shirt and heave-hoed. Soon they had them all back on *terra firma*.

Now it was time for the cautionary tale. Uncle Johnny was in full flight.

'What would you do if you fell in the pit in the middle of the night? You would really be in the poo, with no one to help you. OK. Listen up! Number One Rule! Day or night, under-tens must all agree to go out and pee or poo in twos! What I mean is – come down here in pairs. Right?' They all nodded their heads in unison.

'Yes, Uncle Johnny!'

The fount of all wisdom, uncle Johnny, had spoken. Will was perfectly happy for big brother John to think he was in charge – as long as the house continued to be theirs.

In 1900, Catherine moved to a small cottage in Commercial Road, on the northern outskirts of Talbot, which she had bought for a song. During the prosperous gold era, the population of Clunes was over six thousand. By the turn of the century, numbers had halved and many of the commercial establishments that used to attend to the needs of miners were now empty. Most of the farriers, blacksmiths, leather merchants and horse-dealers had moved on. Houses were being sold at give-away prices as the population dwindled. Cathy saw this as a chance for a bargain.

How did it all pan out? It was about networking. A friend of a friend, who was in the know. A deceased estate. An old house in need of a lick of paint. Going for a song. Family wanted cash on the knocker. A quick sale. Annie made an offer, delving into the family coffers. Offer accepted by son of deceased widow. Vendor and purchaser overjoyed. Whew!

Cathy gleefully proclaimed:

'Now I know what they mean when they talk about the luck of the Irish! It's a buyer's market, and I've just made a killing!'

In reality it was a shabby, run-down shack, a mile and a half from the centre of Talbot. The best part was that it was her own space – no nappies, no spilt milk, no tantrums. It would do for the moment.

Cathy lasted there two years. There were no shops. There were no locals to connect with. It was a long walk to the town centre. She had the company of youngest daughter Ellen who was unmarried, unhappy, and who had moved in with her mum. It wasn't the best of combinations.

Two years later, 1902, Benjamin, the youngest son like the biblical Benjamin, was waiting in the wings to offer company and support to mother Cathy in her old age. Now a mature thirty, he had found the love of his life – the affable, adaptable, hard-working Ada Lillah, or Lillah for short. They did the obvious and natural thing in what had become an essentially law-abiding society. The gold rush was over. People wanted security in the traditional manner. They married and for the first six months they lived with their in-laws.

Lillah's current job was selling women's wear in her father's female apparel shop, in fact, a lingerie store. Ben's philosophy in life was – when you have conflicting issues in life, you compromise.

'Let's swap jobs,' he suggested to Lillah. 'You look after Mum and I'll sell undies.'

Mr Osborne, Lillah's father, had other ideas.

'Benny my boy. I am now about to extend my interests to men's wear. How about we offer you a job in the men's underwear department – calico drawers – long and short, vests, nightshirts, nightcaps and hosiery. A wonderful opportunity for an ambitious young man like you! You never know; if you work hard, one day you may finish up taking over from me.'

Ben thought about it for a moment. He had this other vision of selling drawers and brassieres to uxorious females. But no, that would be but a pipe dream, in any case, probably forbidden by law. And people would talk. Men's undies would have to do.

'OK, Mr Osborne. It's a deal!'

Ben was a lateral thinker. He had another idea. He approached Cathy with his idea.

'Mum, there's a big house for sale in Bond Street, right in the heart of Talbot, near shops and people of all ages. The asking price is reasonable, given the economy at the moment. You and Ellen could move in with Lillah and me. We sell your house, Lillah and I have our savings, and there's a good chance the father-in-law might kick in to make up the difference. What do you think?'

Cathy did think, for a full ten minutes, before asking Ellen. 'What are your thoughts, Ellen?'

'Sounds good to me. I'm sick of wearing out my shoe leather traipsing into Talbot when we need a billy of milk. The milko has never been interested in the industrial area.'

Cathy responded, 'OK. Let's do it!' And they did.

Fortunately, as they surmised, the father-in-law was only too happy to make a contribution to their enterprise.

Lillah was no oil painting, but she had a heart of gold. The main thing was that it was a match that worked. Ellen began to spark up. Cathy smiled contentedly. Lillah was happy to swap selling ladies' underwear with managing the house. Keeping floors spick and span and making cakes was a welcome change from dealing with fussy middle-age matrons who discussed *ad nauseam* the size, style, shape and colour of their smalls.

The bonus was that Cathy, the matriarch, thoroughly approved. Cathy was the main contributor towards the accommodation. Benjamin, as the breadwinner, was responsible for on-going living expenses. During the day he worked in the father-in-law's shop selling men's underwear and accessories. At night he returned to wife and mother, sat down by the fire, perused the *Northern Star*, smoked his pipe, and dined on such luxuries as stewed rabbit, lamb chops and potato in its multiple guises.

Amenities in the 1900s were non-existent. Houses provided a place to sleep and eat and protection from the elements. There was no electricity, running water or sewerage. You were lucky if you had a water-tank. Stormwater drains were non-existent. In towns like Talbot, fortunately you had the services of the 'night-man' who arrived once a week in the dead of night to collect the night soil.

It is really about what you are used to. You take on life's challenges head-on and work around them without whinging. The new house was perfect for all including the grandchildren when it was deemed useful or necessary for them to stay over. The kids enjoyed the chance to spend time with Granny Cath, Uncle Ben and Aunty Lillah and even crotchety old Aunt Ellen.

There was a small snug kitchen, with a woodstove and a narrow space for a kitchen table designed for four. At a pinch you could squash up enough for six, provided they weren't too broad in the beam. The grandkids loved staying over with Granny Cath, which meant hidey, chasey, treasure hunts for lollies, wrestles for the boys, jiving for the girls, impromptu concerts with singing and dancing for all, in the dim light of hurricane lanterns dangling from the walls. On special occasions like birthdays, Granny Cath joined in and sang in a tremulous voice, 'When Irish eyes are smiling.' The kids took their turn with, 'Click go the shears', off the note but with great gusto, in their raucous, soprano voices. Then it was sweet dreams for all till the rooster chorus started early in the morning.

As the years went by, Cathy's health began to deteriorate, though she wasn't prepared to admit it. She was still the resilient potato famine survivor. She was as tough as old boots and did not want to concede to the inevitable debilitating effect of aging. She still cooked, swept and tended the garden. But digging, hoeing and mattocking left her breathless. She had to rest frequently on the tree-stump in the middle of her backyard garden.

Cathy was now seventy-five. If you survived to seventy-five in that era, you were seen as really old. Cathy was constantly wracked with arthritic pain. Ellen, the youngest of James' children and still unmarried at thirty-seven, had learnt to accept the vagaries of communal living. The foursome of Cathy, Ellen, Ben and Lillah worked tolerably well despite the inevitable competition between the three women. Ellen did the ironing, knitting of jumpers and darning of socks. Lillah scrubbed the floors, emptied the rubbish, and attended to the insatiable hunger of the hearth. Cathy cooked the potatoes and sausages, washed the dishes, created the vegie garden, and planted the snapdragons and poppies.

At night after a simple repast, they would sit around the fireplace, retelling their stories and sipping tea. During their odd moments, they chatted with the neighbours and minded the grandchildren as needed. Cathy was toey, being so used to productively labouring on the farm. During the day, despite her weary bones, she still led by example, whenever a little not-too-hard graft was required.

During her idle moments, she soon fell seamlessly into the habit of engaging in small talk with neighbours Mary O'Connor, Beth O'Dwyer and Maureen McClaren. They chatted endlessly about the likelihood of rain, their amazing extended families, the men in their lives, the price of meat and vegies, those confounded hard-working Chinese, her two marriages and the grandkids, not to mention the old stories about the Potato Famine and the workhouse.

As the family proliferates, it is clear that who's who and how they connect with each other is becoming more complicated. In the interests of deobfuscation, it's time to put the rest of the story into the proverbial nutshell!

Annie and J.E. Barrett and their connection with the instigator, researcher and the teller of this story (the two Margarets and myself) have already been dealt with. For the moment we can put that to rest.

*We now concentrate on the remaining main players and how
their lives panned out from the beginning of the twentieth century till
Cathy's demise. At the risk of repetition, we forthwith recap.*

JOHN

1900. John continued to manage the farm assisted by his younger brothers and sisters. He was the boss by seniority and inheritance. He had moved into a granny flat beside the house. He wanted his own space. He continued to be strong-willed and, provided they recognised him as the boss, there was no conflict. He and the affable, hard-working Will worked well together, managing cattle, the orchard and the market garden, assisted by Martha, Mary and Sarah, who continued to work assiduously – until they got a better offer – like matrimony! John remained a confirmed old bachelor.

SARAH

1901. It happened with a rush. Sarah, the youngest and now twenty-five, was the first to leave – in the arms of the worthy Michael Hudson de Medeci. They sanctified their marriage in St Paul's Anglican Church in 1901. Michael was of the upper crust – a man of honour and duty – stiff, starchy and loyal to God, King, Country . . . and, for good measure, Family. They set up house in Annie's hometown, Clunes. The offspring came thick and fast: two boys – Norman, 1902, and Eric, 1904, followed by two girls – Constance, 1906, and Doreen, 1908, at strict carefully regimented intervals.

Sarah continued to be in regular contact with her two older sisters, Martha and Mary, as future events will reveal ...

*We need to move into the future to complete the Michael Hudson
story. As a certain politician said, 'Life was never meant to be easy.'
Sometimes duty comes before the comforts of life, or so Michael*

Hudson de Medeci thought. At the advanced age of thirty-nine years, he enlisted in the army. Twelve months later, May 1915, he found himself in a trench at Gallipoli assailed by machine gun fire and mortar shells. When the whistle blew, he was the first out of the trenches, and he was the first to fall in a hail of bullets. A sad end for a hero – another of history's de Medeci legends!

Sarah never married again. She brought up her four children with memories of their brave father, of whom they were inordinately proud. His body never made it home. Sarah set up a memorial tombstone of her own behind the house. Every Sunday after church service at St Paul's, she and the children would take ten minutes to solemnly remember their wonderful, heroic husband and father.

✝

LEST WE FORGET

MICHAEL HUDSON DE MEDECI. R.I.P.

BENJAMIN

1902. You will undoubtedly remember the Benjamin story. Benjamin at thirty was conflicted between life on the farm and life with a city girl by the name of Ada Lillah. It so happened that Ada Lillah hated cows and vegetables. Ben and Lillah had found common ground. Ben was not particularly interested in life on the farm. He would leave that to John and Willy. Ben was now thirty years old. He had waited long enough. This might be his last chance. Lillah won! They tied the knot.

Lillah's parents owned a men's and women's clothing store. Benjamin joined the firm. So different from eradicating weeds, pumping water and spreading cow manure! Benjamin and Ada Lillah celebrated their union in the traditional Kirby/Lawson way – generating offspring, as it happened, in double figures.

WILLIAM ANDREW

1904. Willy like John was wedded to the farm. He was now thirty-five. Surely it was too late. The cream of the local talent had already been skimmed off. Being picky, it looked as though Will was destined to be a farmer bachelor like brother John. But then the thunderbolt happened, striking him mid-ships in the person of Emily Taylor. It was a Clunes Market romance all over again, very similar to the Annie and E.J. Barrett story.

They had run out of carrots at the farm and Cathy had asked Willy to purchase five pounds of carrots for the family table. Willy left his tomatoes and beans stall to look after themselves trusting to the innate honesty of the Talbot residents. So off he went determined to strike a good deal on the five pounds of carrots.

He soon discovered that he had met his match in the person of Emily Taylor at her carrot stall.

'Hi Miss. What's yer best price on five pound of carrots?'

'Tuppence a pound, sir.'

Hoping to assert his male dominance Willy responded.

'Ridiculous!'

'Take it or leave it, sir!'

Willy was nothing if not quick.

'Penny halfpenny a pound or nothing!'

'It looks like it's nothing, sir!'

What a way to begin a romance!

'OK. You win! You're good! I know when I'm beaten. Here's your ten pence for the five pound of carrots.'

'Thank you, Sir!'

Willy had not finished.

'How would you like to work for me, selling vegies?'

'Sorry sir. I treasure my independence.'

'No problem! You can run the stall when I'm away at the farm.'

How could she resist?

That's how it began. Late 1904, they tied the knot.

MARY

It was now Mary's turn. Mary was easy-going, affable, chilled out and gregarious, like Jesus' friend Mary. Two years later, 1906, at the age of thirty-two, Mary married George Romey. They took up residence in Maryborough and produced a daughter, Olethea Laurie, in the same year, 1906. Olethea was to be their only child, apparently as a result of birthing complications.

It seems that the name Olethea was the flavour of the month. Younger sister Sarah had a daughter at the same time whom she named Alethea Constance, with an A instead of an O. It seems that there was a little game-playing between the sisters. Mary won the sisterly duel, with Sarah agreeing to use the name Constance, with Alethea being her second name.

MARTHA

Biblically speaking, you couldn't have a Mary without a Martha. Of course, Martha was the workaholic, married to hard graft in the kitchen. She was forever scrubbing floors, baking cakes and washing dishes. No time to waste in idle chatter! Mary and Martha were good friends nevertheless, respecting each other's propensities. There was a four-year difference in their ages, Martha being the elder.

Martha, now thirty-six years of age, had almost given up on the prospect of matrimony. She had little time for socialising. David Henson was on the look-out for a prospective bride who would look after him in style, who could produce cakes with lemon icing, cook spuds and chops to perfection, and who could keep a house clean and tidy. Martha fitted the bill. David was handsome, generous, yes, but at the same time he was fixated on the prospect of a no-hassle household.

It was a perfect match. They had no time to waste given her age. No hanky panky in those days! So a month later they sanctified their love in holy matrimony.

Within four years they had three delightful offspring. If only it was always so easy!

AN INTERESTING THOUGHT!

Genealogies mean all kinds of things to different people, depending on the kind of mind-set you are blessed with. For person A, for whom the present is what matters, genealogies can be an uninteresting succession of unknown or long forgotten names that they don't know and are not particularly interested in. For person B, your genealogy can represent a fascinating life story with yourself at the pinnacle.

From Cathy to our grandchildren – Grace, Sophie, Jesse, James and Ben – we have seven generations. They are somewhere along the bottom line of a seven-generation triangle.

Theoretically, if we all followed Cathy's example, with all of her progeny generating thirteen children each over seven generations, having recourse to exponential mathematics, we would finish up with 62,748,517 children.

That's a lot of children!

If on the other hand, you average a mere five children per family, theoretically you might finish up with a mere 371,293 children.

And if we follow the modern trend of maybe two children per family, your tally might be a paltry zero. Yes, indeed – an interesting thought! We can only surmise. The fact is that we don't possess a grand total that includes all of our distant relatives.

To keep it simple I shall confine myself to the direct line. If you find genealogies, even the short version, tedious, skip the next page. If you like general pictures, you may be happy like me to accept a truncated version:

Six generations ago, I PETER HALL had a great-great-grandmother called Cathy (Potato famine orphan), then a great-grandmother called Annie Barrett, a granny called Alice, a dad called Cliff, and here I am. I have one wife, Marie, three children and five grandchildren, and that's it!

Likewise, my two fellow descendants, both MARGARETS, who aided and abetted in the telling of this simple tale, share the same great-grandmother as myself, namely Annie. We are second cousins (I think).

MARGARET WALSHE had a grandmother called Eliza Mabel Barrett, a mother called Vera, and has a husband called Bernie. They have four children and eleven grandchildren.

MARGARET VRKLJAN had a grandmother called Kathleen Isabella Barrett, a mother called Alma, and a husband called Rocco. As far as I know, they have two children and two grandchildren.

The three of us are second cousins.

CATHERINE – the potato famine orphan, is my focus. The rest is for another story by someone else at another time.

Cathy's Final Days

We are now approaching the end of the Cathy Kirby/Lawson story. Cathy was now eighty-three years of age. Quite remarkable in an era when the average life span for a woman was around forty years. Cathy had survived the deaths of father, mother, four siblings, two husbands and five children. Her life has been an admixture of sadness, joy, hard work, determination and triumph. Finally, on 29 September, thirteen years after the allotted span of three score and ten, Cathy slipped off to meet her maker – presumably God – aided and abetted four score and three years previously by parents Andrew O'Laughlan and Mary Kelly.

Putting Catherine's final days into a wider context, we go back to 28 July 1914, two months before her death. On that day, one of the most devastating wars in history erupted, with Germany, Britain and France at the epicentre. After years of muscle-flexing, economic rivalry and simmering tensions between Germany and Britain, what was essentially a trade war broke out. The pretext was the assassination in Sarajevo of Archduke Ferdinand, the presumptive heir of the Austro-Hungarian

Empire. For no convincing reason, the new concept of a world war was to become a reality.

World War I, also known as the Great War or the War to End All Wars, was eventually to involve over a hundred countries. Australia was dragged into this conflict by the fact that we were a colony of Great Britain. The irony was that thousands of young men lusting for travel and excitement and driven by a newfound surge of patriotism were hankering for a fight for a cause. Disillusionment came later. Nevertheless, we Australians learnt about the honour of dying for a cause, celebrated in the course of such disasters as Gallipoli and Villers-Bretonneux. The pointless extinction of human life that followed eventually accounted for 18,000,000 lives worldwide. Of these, 60,284 Australians were among those who died in the conflict.

This crazy turmoil of death and destruction began in Cathy's last two months on this earth. There was no radio or television to inform the populace of what was happening on the worldwide stage. Cathy was unable to access newspapers, as she continued to be stubbornly illiterate. Nevertheless she gleaned information from such sources as family, friends and the marketplace.

What she was particularly interested to know was that the Irish were against this war, primarily because of their historic antipathy towards all that was British. Ingrained in her psyche was the conviction that one million Irish citizens, including her whole family, died in the Potato Famine, deprived by Britain of their land, food and citizenship. Furthermore, her new Irish hero, Archbishop Daniel Mannix, the recently consecrated Catholic archbishop of Melbourne, had embarked on a vitriolic campaign against conscription. This was good enough for Cathy. At eighty-three she still possessed her Irish fire. True to form, very few of her extended family, informed as they were by historic Irish prejudices, offered their services in what they saw as a pointless trade war. The British could do it on their own!

The year of Cathy's death, 1914, was a year of disasters – international, national and familial. Following the pattern, three women, daughters Martha and Mary together with mother Cathy, all from within the close-knit Kirby/Lawson families, departed this life.

The first was Martha. Her sister Mary likewise succumbed that same night, apparently afflicted by the same cause. Their story had a portentous biblical ring about it. Martha Henson loved working in the kitchen churning out cakes and cooking such pedestrian delicacies as sausages and potatoes (what we call bangers and mash), while Mary Romey preferred sitting round for a chat. Like the original Martha and Mary, they were siblings as well as good friends. Tragically, their battle with death occurred within a few hours of each other.

How did it come about? It was about ignorance, inexperience, bad decisions and bad luck.

The three sisters, Martha, forty-four, Mary, forty, and Sarah, thirty-eight, were enjoying a party with their eight children at Mary and George Romey's Maryborough home. Mary and George had one daughter, Olethea Laurie, aged six. Martha and her three children were visiting from their home in Clunes, about twenty miles away. Sarah had also joined them from her Stoney Creek cottage with her four children, Norman, Eric, Constance and Doreen.

Given that they had eight exuberant children between them, it was party time – fun and games in the bush behind the family home. Late afternoon, the kids came home with a stash of mushrooms, which they had discovered under an oak-tree in the paddock behind their house. Martha and Mary, who didn't know much about mushrooms, innocently assumed they were ordinary innocuous field mushrooms, just perfect for mushrooms on toast. They were mistaken. Martha and Mary were the only ones to partake. The mushrooms were in fact of the *death cap* variety – *amanita phalloides*.

Soon after ingesting these innocent-looking fungi, they began to experience stomach pains, nausea, vomiting and diarrhoea. They both became seriously ill over the next eight days.

This time it was a battle with death by poisoning, not childbirth, the most common cause of women's deaths in that era. They assumed it was ordinary gastro, and they were ready to tough it out. A bad decision! Martha departed this life eight days after partaking of those innocent-looking fungi. Mary joined her that same night.

Their four surviving children were inconsolable. One day they had their dear, fun-loving mothers; eight days later they were bereft, desolate and motherless.

Olethea Laurie, daughter of George and Mary and an only child felt totally abandoned. To lose both her mother and her favourite, fun-loving aunt was too much for a six-year old to take in.

Martha's thee children were similarly devastated. But at least they had each other and their dad.

George Romey and David Henson, grieving husbands and fathers, had the unenviable task of consoling their four grieving children and, at the same time, continuing to run a household and also earn a living. This was the era of the stiff upper lip. Death was a reoccurring, inevitable reality. You grieve, you weep, and then you get on with life.

David and George agreed that whatever happened, their children must not be burdened with a guilt trip. They stifled their own grief and gathered the children together. David spoke: 'Your mother is now in heaven where we will all join her one day. What happened was a fearful accident. None of us knew that poisonous mushrooms sometimes grow under oak trees. None of us had ever heard of death cap mushrooms. And your mothers hadn't either.'

George, the younger of the two grieving husbands added: 'No one is to blame. It was an unfortunate accident. We'll weep together for your dear mums and loving aunts, and my beautiful wife and wonderful sister-in-law, but just remember – no one is to blame. We have our special memories and we will live our lives as well as we can, just as they would want us to. Both of them will remain in our hearts forever, and we'll all join them one day.' George and David were not used to embracing each other, but they did on this occasion, enfolding the whole family together physically and emotionally in a bond that would ensure their survival.

The sad news reached Cathy by Cobb and Co coach the following day. Daughter Ellen deciphered the telegram for her still illiterate mum. Cathy had lived through the death of siblings, parents, two husbands and now, counting Martha and Mary, five children. But she never got used to it. John drove Cathy on the rough, twenty-mile, bone-crunching ride to Maryborough for the funeral. As we already know, in that era with its lack of refrigeration, funerals had to occur the day after death.

You would think that Cathy at the age of eighty-three would have been accustomed to the non-discriminatory reality of death. Over the years, she had survived the deaths of thirteen loved ones. But you never get used to it. She struggled to rein in her emotions. Her thoughts went back to the orphanage sixty-seven years ago, when her own family died of starvation and disease during the Potato Famine. She had had her share of sadness. Mothers don't expect to survive their children. It was all too much. So she surrendered to the emotion of the moment in the predictable fashion.

The funeral happened at St Augustine's Catholic Church, Maryborough. Communal grief is one of those things you can't contain. And why should you? It's a cathartic release valve that enables us to continue our lives when our grief is spent.

They held the wake at the Romey family home, reminiscing, telling the old stories that began with 'Remember the day when ...' There was a dull ache in their hearts, sad smiles on their lips, and determination to make the most of their lives on the inside as well as the outside, just as their wonderful mums would have wanted.

Their immediate task was to work out a plan for the future about child-minding, household chores and school. Whatever happened, Sarah and her brood of four were ready to help out. No easy task, as the two bereft fathers had to return to work to ensure the financial survival of their respective families.

Three days later, Cathy, now quite feeble, struggled to breathe as John helped her climb back on to the old cart. Soon they were clip-clopping their way back to Talbot.

Sarah De Medeci, the youngest and the sole survivor of the three sisters, was now the mother of eight. Sarah's Protestant husband, Michael, a devoted fan of Billy Hughes, the conscription advocate, was away fighting the Axis forces. Billy Hughes, despised by Irish Catholics and opposed by the inveterate Irish Archbishop Mannix, tried in vain to have his conscription laws introduced in Australia. Mannix described the First World War as a trade war and vigorously opposed conscription. Nevertheless, there were enough young Australian men, mainly Protestant, who were ready to enlist. Sarah as the good wife supported her husband's sense of patriotism, but that did not make it easier on the home front if you had four young children to feed and care for, as well as the extra four from Martha and Mary.

Sarah and the two husbands did their best in an impossible situation, given that Michael Hudson De Medeci was in Egypt with the Australian armed forces, preparing to embark for Gallipoli. For the rest of the year, Sarah and her four children remained in Maryborough to help out. For the moment, seven of the eight children attended St Mary's local Catholic school, accounting for six hours each day, Monday to Friday. But when they arrived back home at four o'clock, tired and grumpy, after a hard day of reading and writing and arithmetic, under the demanding eyes of their 'take-no-prisoners' teachers, it was utter mayhem. Enough to elicit tears of frustration, angry tantrums, and the application of the feather duster!

To add to the tragedy, twelve months later (as we already know), fate struck another sickening blow. They were the recipients of that dreaded telegram. Michael De Medeci had died in the trenches at Gallipoli. Of the original six parents, we now have only three to pick up the pieces.

Cathy, meanwhile, was continuing to fail despite her fighting spirit. In addition to the debilitating effect of old age, she had to deal with repeated bouts of bronchial asthma. They say that the secret to achieving a ripe old age is to 'keep on breathing'. Breathing was Cathy's over-riding challenge, given the suffocating nature of bronchial asthma. A British war was the least of her concerns.

Five of her children had already departed this life over the last forty-one years. They included Mary Anne (cot death, 1852), Catherine (puerperal sepsis, 1878), Eliza Jane (child-birth, 1893), Martha and Mary (death-cap fungus poisoning, 1914). The men were the survivors. Child-birth continued to be a major cause of death for women. Being female seemed to be a life-limiting condition. The average age for women at this time was forty. Fortunately, childbearing had never been a problem for Cathy. She was haunted by other demons, like old age. She no longer tended her peas and poppies much less her potatoes in the garden behind the house. But her mind continued to function adequately despite mild memory loss. Bronchial asthma was her one serious affliction.

Mid-September, Catherine was admitted to Amherst Hospital, suffering from an extreme case of bronchial asthma. Her symptoms were severe coughing fits that wracked her worn-out body together with spasms of asthmatic wheezing and shortness of breath. Her attending physician was Dr P. D. Cunningham. After ten fruitless days in hospital, Dr Cunningham regretfully informed Cathy that there was little more he could do for her. Cathy wheezed out her thanks with a wry, accepting smile. 'Thanks, Doctor Cunningham. I just want to go home.'

Faithful old Naggy trotted along the bumpy track with

John at the reins. Three miles and one hour later, Cathy was back home at Bond Street with ever-faithful unmarried daughter Ellen Kirby, her half-brother Ben and his wife Lillah.

Her grand-daughter, Ellen Sainsbury and husband John Hallinan were over for a visit from Stoney Creek. By marriage, she was now Ellen Hallinan. Having two Ellens in the one house made it confusing. They became Ellen H and Ellen K. Despite her resistance to booklearning, Cathy had now under sufferance learnt two letters of the alphabet.

Putting the two Ellens into context, we have Cathy's unmarried daughter, Ellen Kirby, who had lived with her for the last fourteen years, and there was Ellen Hallinan (Sainsbury), her grand-daughter and mover and shaker. Grand-daughter Ellen was the daughter of Elizabeth and William Sainsbury, dyed-in-the wool Methodists. Work that out if you can! And if you can't, it doesn't matter.

William was a legend at Stoney Creek. He was the local blacksmith, known for his reliability as well as his crustiness. He worked in his forge from dawn till dusk, pumping his enormous cowhide bellows, infusing white-hot heat to his coals, shaping horseshoes and frying pans for his customers.

To William the blacksmith's disgust, his daughter Ellen turned Catholic when she married John Hallinan, whom he barely tolerated. 'This is the bloke who turned my daughter into a Mick.' Like her father, Ellen was stubborn and unmovably fixated on whatever goal she set her energies to. She adored Grandma Cath and was determined to visit her whenever she had the chance. Stubbornness and loyalty were shared characteristics. So why shouldn't she become a Catholic like her Granny, no matter what her Methodist dad had to say – particularly as she now visited her gran so often and stayed over quite frequently?

Being a Catholic was an identity frequently associated with Irish ancestry. It was not always accompanied by a churchgoing mindset, despite the thunderings from the pulpit about hellfire and brimstone for

Catholics who did not regularly attend Sunday Mass. Cathy had not attended church during her marriage to James mainly because at that time there was no Catholic Church in the vicinity of Clunes. They made a special effort for weddings. Kirby family marriages were celebrated at St Francis' Church, in the city of Melbourne.

During her marriage to George, Cathy had continued to be non-church-going because of her ambivalent, unmarried, 'sinful' status. It was sorted out when they were married on his deathbed. It was a compromise marriage, being neither Catholic nor Anglican. It was celebrated, as you may or may not remember, on 1 June 1883 by Bible Christian Church minister, Reverend William Bitten. Cathy was now officially married in the eyes of the state, albeit at the hands of a non-Catholic minister. In her own eyes she was still a Catholic.

The main difficulty for Irish Catholics who lived and worked in the goldfields was the lack of Catholic priests and Catholic churches. They became non-church-going Catholics because of the 'tyranny of distance' as Geoffrey Blainey would have said. Now there was no excuse because St Mary's Catholic Church, Talbot, had become a reality. It was situated at 15 Heales Street, just around the corner from Cathy's Camp Street home. Till recently, she would pop around the corner for Sunday Mass, bringing with her whatever other members of the family she had managed to cajole into keeping her company.

The Lawson family of Bond Street, Talbot, now numbered five adults. There was Ben the haberdashery salesman and homebody wife Lillah who now had a brood of three energetic children, and there was unmarried sister Ellen who had learned to smile again, and eighty-two-year-old grandmother Cathy. During her Commercial Road sojourn, she had really missed the house full of children. What's more, Bond Street continued to be convenient for all being close to shops and work.

Unmarried sister Ellen had a distinct aversion for the appellation *spinster.* She insisted that *spinning* was one of her least favourite pastimes. She wanted to be known as *sister* or *aunty.* In her role as Aunty Ellen she revelled in sharing in the role of baby feeder, bather, nappy changer and nappy washer. Aunty Ellen now had a permanent smile on her face.

As for Cathy, she had missed the hustle and bustle of family life during her two-year sojourn in Commercial Road. The Bond Street vibe was so different. The kids would crawl up on to her knee for a cuddle, calling out 'Horsey! Horsey!' Cathy would sadly respond 'Sorry kids! I can't do Horsey these days. My poor old knees don't work too well. You'll have to ask Da when he gets home!' All she could do was potter around the house and every few days check on the potato crop in the back garden. 'They should be ready in another month. I'll get Ben to dig 'em up. Then it'll be spuds, spuds and more spuds!'

Meanwhile the Bond Street contingent was joined by the other Ellen – Ellen Sainsbury – now Ellen Hallinan following her marriage to John Hallinan. Her dad, William Sainsbury, blacksmith and devoted member of the Primitive Methodist Church, took some time to accept Roman Catholic John Hallinan into his family. It was even harder when young Ellen decided to give away Methodism to become a Catholic. They finally made peace when he discovered that Johnny H was a shoer of horses, making him a kind of blacksmith. Ellen H was totally fascinated by Cathy's Potato Famine orphan story and saw her as a heroine to emulate. She formed a close bond with Grandma Cath whom she visited as often as she could.

House prices in Talbot continued to fall. Fortuitously, the house next door to the Lawson Bond Street home suddenly popped up on the market. Young Ellen pounced. 'How about it John? Great house! Great price! Next to Grandma Cath's.' Fortunately husband John caved in and the deal was done. They moved in next door to the Lawsons in September 1914.

Old age eventually gets the better of us. Despite her determination and resilience, Cathy was beginning to fail. Father O'Grady from St Mary's would regularly visit her with Communion and a blessing. The end was indeed near. Cathy knew it.

Young Ellen visited Catherine every day. The children wanted to clamber all over Cathy, whether she was in her favourite armchair or resting in bed. It was all too much. A communal decision was made, despite Cathy's protestations, to move her in next door to the Hallinan house. Young Ellen became the self-appointed nursemaid. Day and night she was at Catherine's beck and call. How can you cough and smile and wheeze at the same time? But that's what happened. They were soul-mates.

It was early afternoon, Saturday 12 September 1914. Cathy called the family over in the hope of being able to express her final farewell. Asthma and bronchial issues had taken their toll. They gathered around – her eight remaining children, their spouses and her grandchildren. Cathy tried with moderate success to supress her coughing with the aid of the latest remedy, bitrate of tar – recommended by Doctor P. D. Cunningham.

John was in charge. He hushed the muted whisperings with a wave of his hand. They were all lined up in two ranks with the children at the front. An ominous silence reigned. Cathy tried in vain to smile and struggled for breath as she strove between gasps to huskily whisper her final words.

Ellen Hallinan, the bossy granddaughter, competed with John, hushing them all as Cathy strove to make herself heard. No wonder Ellen became a schoolteacher later on at the Stoney Creek School (No. 886), where she was as uncompromising with her schoolkids as she was with her family.

Catherine suddenly became unexpectedly coherent. Her memory didn't miss a beat – names, connections, down to the humble potato.

'I'm so proud of you all … and I love you to bits … sons and daughters and grand-sons and grand-daughters … in-laws too … the whole damn lot of you! It's been a great life … I am off to join my own mum Mary and dad Andrew … and my brothers and sisters Brigid, Eamon, Brendan, Deidre … and my dear hubbies, James and George … my departed girls who left in a rush … Mary Anne, Catherine, Eliza Jane, Martha and Mary … And as for all of you in-laws and grand-kids … I'll see you in heaven!

'Johnny, you're in charge now … Marg, Liz, Annie, Ellen, Willy, Ben and Sarah, I know you'll do me proud. Keep them potatoes coming … Spuds kept my family alive in Ireland … till they turned black … Without them my family would have died … Just remember … you wouldn't be here without spuds … No spuds, no me, no you!

'That's it! I'm out of puff …"

Catherine closed her eyes and seemed to be at peace. It was Saturday 12 September 1914.

They agreed to let her sleep. Most went on their way, taking the children home. Remaining on watch were Ben, his wife Ada Lillah, and faithful grand-daughter Ellen Sainsbury-Hallinan and her husband

That same night, shortly before midnight, Cathy was shaken by another coughing spasm, accompanied by a suffocating asthmatic attack. Her weakened heart and lungs pumped in vain as she tried to breathe. It was too much. It was time. She died of a heart attack, verified by Dr P. D. Cunningham.

Thus was Cathy's departure from this life officially recorded:

— CERTIFICATE OF DEATH —

This is to acknowledge the death of:

CATHERINE LAWSON (KIRBY) – née O'LAUGHLAN

On the 12th day of September, in the year 1914

At Talbot, Victoria

Signed: P. D. Cunningham (M.D.)

There were a few tears but not too many. Cathy's life was a life to be celebrated, not to be wept over. And that's how her funeral was defined – a celebration of the life of a remarkable woman, whom they loved, admired and thanked right to the end.

Catherine had been coherent to her last breath. It had been an uncomfortable but not an unduly painful death. Cathy accepted that it was time to go. She had come to terms with the tragic deaths of her Irish family. She thanked God for her two good husbands, her thirteen children, and she felt reasonably sure that she would meet them somewhere, some time, between here and eternity.

Cathy's coffin took pride of place at the end of the dining room. The coffin was open. Her eyes were more or less closed. There was a glint from the left eye, which seemed slightly more open than its companion.

'I think Mum is winking at us', whispered John to Willy.

Willy's response was, 'I think she's checking up on us to make sure we do her wake in the proper Irish way!'

Cathy was dressed in her Sunday gear. Her complexion was pale. Her wrinkles had somehow ironed themselves out. Her lips looked bloodless with the slightest suggestion of a beatific Mona Lisa kind of smile. She seemed to exude the message, 'Chill out, my darlings. Death is not that bad. I needed a rest after a hard life putting up with you lot. So relax. We'll catch up again one day!'

Margaret had managed to rustle up Cathy's old wedding dress from a dusty cupboard where it had survived the moths and the weevils over the years. She shook out the dust and ironed it as best she could with the chunky flat-iron which she heated on the wood stove.

It was a typical Irish wake – emotional speeches, clinking and breaking of glassware, generous quantities of the good stuff, slurred voices, a barrel of Aussie lager, a spot of poteen, sentimental Irish songs, favourite memories, the oft-repeated yarns. Cathy was elevated to the status of saint, the best mother in the history of creation, amazing cook – amazing everything. Her roast beef was legendary.

John declared with deep emotion: 'She was the most fantastic mum ever. She washed our bums and smacked 'em when we needed it. She hugged us, growled at us, encouraged us, yelled at us in style. Yeah, she was the best mum in creation.'

Not to be outdone, William Andrew took the floor: 'Come on, one and all! Charge yer glasses and down the hatch! To the most amazing mum ever!'

Hers was a life to be celebrated rather than unduly mourned. She had undoubtedly gone to her reward, reposing in the bosom of Abraham, embracing Jesus, hugging Mary and her namesake St Catherine of Siena, not to mention those thirteen family members who had gone before her.

By two o'clock, most had gone home. The immediate family watched and prayed till first light. John and Benjamin closed the coffin as dawn broke. The ever-trusty Naggy transported Cathy in the creaking cart to St Mary's Catholic Church for the early morning service. It was just around the corner in Heales Street. The September weather was cool enough to allow a day and a half time lapse between death and burial. The funeral service was to take place that morning at 8.00 o'clock.

Bleary-eyed family and friends installed themselves in the rough-hewn wooden pews, determined to give Cathy an appropriate send-off. This was one occasion when Father O'Grady's favourite sermon about hell-fire and brimstone was totally inappropriate. He spoke about God's mercy, His love for big families and devoted mothers, the tough life in the goldfields, overcoming death and adversity, the welcoming angels in the heavens, and God's reward for saintly Irish Catholics like Cathy.

Finally, the funeral cortege, headed by Naggy and his dray, transporting Cathy in her coffin and followed by family and friends on foot, wended its way to the Amherst Cemetery. The gravediggers had been out the day before preparing for yet another burial. It had meant six hard hours digging into the unforgiving clay. But they were used to it. All was ready when the cortege arrived.

The mourners stood solemnly around the coffin, which reposed above the gaping hole, supported by two four by twos. Father O'Grady spoke his ritual words:

> *Into your hands, Father of mercies,*
> *we commend our sister Catherine,*
> *in the sure and certain hope*
> *that, together with all who have died in Christ,*
> *she will rise with Him on the last day.*

The wooden supports were removed. It was hand over hand on the ropes. The coffin bumped its way to its resting place. Clumps of earth reverberated on the lid of coffin. Tears began to flow and the silence was broken by repressed sobs from both man and woman. It was time to go. Sad smiles and whispered conversations resumed, and soon all was back to normal.

Life goes on!

✝

R.I.P.
CATHERINE O'LAUGHLAN/KIRBY/LAWSON

TO ROUND IT OFF

This story was a journey that started several years ago. At that stage I had completed much of my research and roughed out the first two pages. Then came the stroke. As I slowly emerged from the haze, I looked at those two pages and decided, regretfully, that to continue would be impossible. Two years later, and following many restless nights, I realised that there was no such thing as impossible. Why not give it a go?

I contacted Margaret and Bernard Walshe and discovered in them two very affirming friends who were prepared to help by researching a variety of historical resources as well as making available their stash of relevant photos. Twelve months later I emerged with a completed Cathy story. Marzie (my dear wife whose real name is Marie) helped with a first effort at editing the text, sorting our facts, names and sequencing.

I researched available photos from galleries, family files and the Internet, supplementing those supplied by Marg and Bernie, thus adding a certain life and energy to the story. We were now ready to go.

Next, I called upon the services of our friend David Lovell, publisher and editor supremo with an eagle eye for detail. David meticulously researched the story for the inevitable blips and inconsistencies. And, to top it off, for a final cut and polish, I availed myself of the services of our son Simon, an experienced wordsmith, who applied his writing skills and eye for detail to the final draft. Thanks Si.

We were now ready to make the dream a reality.

Maybe this humble tome will be a source of entertainment and instruction for all those out there who are exploring their own family stories.

Peter Anthony Hall